Life, Love, and Baseball

Also by D.K. Godard

Non-fiction with Skyler Wolf Jones
From Dude to Dad: The Only Guide a Dude Needs to be a Dad

Life, Love, and Baseball
A Novel

D.K. Godard

Griffin
Publishers

Printed in the United States of America

First Printing: 2009 The Switch Pitcher
Second Edition: 2012 Life, Love, and Baseball

ISBN-13: 978-0-692-47181-4

Griffin Publishers, LLC

www.griffinpublishers.com

Dedication

To Amy, for believing in me when I didn't believe in myself.
To Ms. Kenny-Stein, who opened the door of writing.

-ONE-

It was a warm mid spring afternoon as Jeremy ran to class. There was only one place that he wanted to be right now; it was not his class. As he leapt down steps and over some bushes on campus Jeremy could hear the noises from the diamond dwindle behind him. The faint sound of the cheering crowd told him that the game was closing into a solid victory.

Jeremy flipped out his phone as he narrowly missed a professor and TA. He did not have time to dial as an incoming text chimed. He slowed half a pace so he could read the updated score. The text informed him of a slam to a wide gap in the outfield which allowed two runners in with a man on second; this would certainly be a solid victory. Jeremy smiled as he folded the phone back into his pocket. He released a modest jump as he increased his speed.

He rounded the corner of the final building and slid through the closing glass doors. Jeremy immediately had to change speed when his shoes began to slip over the tile floor. He had not realized that skirting so close to sprinklers on campus would leave so much water and mud stuck to the soles of his shoes. He attempted to stop too quickly before the door to his class and slid beyond the doorway. His fingertips just caught the edge of the door frame as he heard the chuckling of a few of his classmates. He was not sure if they were laughing that he was late yet again or that he had almost missed the door and landed on the ground. Either way, Jeremy feigned composure as he avoided his professor's glare, while sliding into a seat in the middle of the rows of desks.

"Ah, yes. Jeremy. I was wondering when you were going to grace us with your presence," the professor said with a wheeze.

"Sorry Professor," Jeremy panted. "The game went a little long."

"Game? What game?" the professor asked impatiently.

"Baseball, sir," supplied Jeremy.

"A baseball game?" asked the professor with a huff. "Couldn't you have just recorded it off of the TV?"

"Oh, no sir," Jeremy said with a grin. "It was a home game. Here," Jeremy said as though this should have been apparent. "And," Jeremy paused, while pulling out his chiming phone, "we just struck out their last three at-bats very quickly to finish it off," he said proudly before silencing the phone and returning it to his pocket.

"And you could not wait to read it in the school paper in the morning or get the results from that deplorable device in your pocket," the professor provided as a statement and not a question.

"Oh, no, I have to be there in person when they play at home," Jeremy answered with his grin spreading.

"And risk failing my class?" the professor asked over his chalk dust-tipped glasses.

"Well, yeah," Jeremy said dumbfounded. "It's baseball. It's America's favorite pastime."

"If all my students had that sort of passion for this subject, I would be learning from them," the professor pouted as he turned back to the board.

Jeremy settled into his seat, while pulling out his notebook.

"Now, if you don't mind, Jeremy," the professor said looking over his shoulder as he raised his hand to the board, "With your permission, I would like to get back to my class."

"Uh, sure, no problem. Just remember," Jeremy said looking around at the class, "they play again tomorrow at seven." Jeremy turned back to his incredulous professor and waved him on, "You may continue."

The professor resembled a large mouth bass for a few seconds before spinning back to the board with a muttered "Hurumph."

At just under six feet in height, Jeremy really did seem average. His hair was dirty blond with the same hairstyle he'd had since he was a child; conservatively combed, parted and left to dry. If his hair was not combed, it was because he had succumbed to the need to wear one of his favorite baseball hats. His collection focused on two types. First, he had a small number of fitted hats for his favorite teams over the years that he tried to keep in good condition. His second collection was what he termed "The Historic Collection." These hats were from what he lovingly referred to as hats from the Golden Years of baseball. Some of the hats were past versions of teams that still existed. Others were from old teams that had been moved or renamed. Jeremy loved these hats and did not want to wear them out, as they were harder to replace.

His complexion was just starting to gain the benefits of the return of longer days and warmer weather. If he did not wear hats all the time, then his hair would lighten from the sun and become more boyish. During the winter, Jeremy joked that he was perfecting the art of human hibernation. His mid-section became wider as he packed on some winter weight. His hair even seemed to grow thicker rather than longer in the winters. Jeremy always tried to keep himself reasonably in shape during the year, yet he seemed to maintain the weight that he wanted best during the spring and summer months;

most likely because it was easier to play baseball during those months than in the winter.

In Jeremy's opinion, his most defining attribute was his mind. In his college freshman English class, when asked to describe himself, he wrote, "I feel like my mind has become an iPod Shuffle, set on permanent shuffle; especially when I'm in class." Jeremy tried to pay attention in every class. His desire to do well in his college studies was often thwarted by his active imagination. Jeremy would try to constantly write everything that the professors said or wrote. However, soon, his hand would cramp, and he'd need to stop to rest. Instantly, his mind began to wander into avenues completely unrelated to the subject at hand. Jeremy had never wanted to think of himself as someone with attention deficit, rather someone with too many ideas. In an effort to focus his mind in class, he utilized an experiment he had discovered years before in grade school.

Jeremy had been teased by his first grade teacher for not being able to decide which hand to use when learning how to write. During every exercise they went through in class, Jeremy would switch hands, trying to find which one was more comfortable. Finally, Jeremy followed the example of his older brother and stuck with his left hand. Everyone else in the family wrote with their right, except for his older brother, Nathan. Jeremy wanted to be like Nathan and chose to use his left hand for writing; though Jeremy suspected that Nathan had always resented him for this decision.

A few years later, Jeremy was reminded by his parents of the discussion they had with his teacher about his insistency to switch hands. Jeremy's family noticed that, while he wrote left handed, he did everything else with his right hand. While always labeled a lefty, because of his writing hand, he found some uniqueness in learning to be ambidextrous.

In high school, Jeremy began to learn how many things he could do with either hand. It came in handy in sports to be able to confuse others about which side was stronger. Eventually, certain tasks became equally proficient with either hand. In college, Jeremy began taking his notes in class with his right hand instead of his left. This forced him to focus more on the class, and if his mind wandered, it was usually directed to improving the legibility of his handwriting. Jeremy was trying to focus on his handwriting now, while his professor droned through the rest of the class. This was becoming increasingly difficult as Jeremy became even more ambidextrous.

"Remember a full, detailed analysis of what we have covered for this next test," the professor stirred Jeremy, "due at next class. Oh, and Mr. Chase?" he asked, focusing on Jeremy, "A word if you don't mind."

Jeremy walked slowly up to the front of the class room as the rest of the class hurried out.

"Mr. Chase," the professor said in a patronizing way, "I understand that you have desires elsewhere, but if you plan on passing this class, you need to attend class."

"Yes sir," Jeremy mumbled. "I haven't missed a day."

"That means more than just being here every day," the professor cut in, "It means more than writing furiously in your notes. You need to answer sample questions, participate in class discussion, and act like you have something other than baseball rattling in your head."

"Yes sir."

"You are going to need to stand out in your program if you want to catch the eye of employers," the professor scolded.

Jeremy muttered an agreement.

"That will do. You may go," he said, waving Jeremy out of the room.

Growing up in a family of seven gave each member of the family plenty of opportunities to shine or fade in the light of the other children. While Jeremy's older siblings excelled in school, music, and sports, Jeremy seemed unable to excel in any one area. He was average in every endeavor. He could pick up what he needed to learn just as well as any other student in most subjects. Some subjects or skills required more effort for Jeremy than for the rest of his classes. He was always able to eventually adapt and be with everyone else. It frustrated him that his older siblings did not seem to need as much time to pick up anything. They were model students and talented athletes. Jeremy followed in their paths in school and sports but never matched their ability. He quickly learned that he would need to find something to help him stand out from the group, if he was ever to be recognized.

Years later, at college, Jeremy was still average. He knew that he should not feel ashamed being average, yet, an average student, in an average under graduate degree would not stand out to employers as being worth the time to interview. Jeremy understood that if he wanted to rise above average, he would have to be able to pay better attention while in class. Jeremy had reached a point that his only motivation for attending his classes was so he could hopefully find a way to be unique.

-TWO-

Like most young adults who graduate from high school, Jeremy wanted to put a considerable distance between himself and his parents for college. Jeremy's family had lived most of their time in Salem, Massachusetts. The bay weather and the cold winters took a physical toll on the inhabitants of Salem, especially his parents. Jeremy said his parents looked as though the wind and oppressive cold had permanently shaped them into scowling hunches that barked at everything Jeremy or his siblings did that was against their parental designs.

Jeremy's graduation from high school seemed to signify to his parents that it was now acceptable to move to a more hospitable climate. The weekend that Jeremy started his freshman year of college, his parents moved the rest of the family down to south Texas. They had begun to act as though they had been forced to live in Salem for Jeremy's benefit. Now that he was gone, his parents acted as though they were free to move. Jeremy wondered how long this move would last, as southern Texas was one of the last places you'd expect to find shrewd New Englanders, but, his parents seemed to be happy now that they were away from the cold and harsh wind of the Massachusetts Bay area.

There was one main reason why Jeremy did not like that his parents now lived in Texas; they were only half a continent away. If they had stayed in Salem, he could have been separated from them by the whole country. His one advantage was that his school was cradled in the mountains with lots of snow and cold. He knew when making his decision about college, he would have to pick a location that his parents would be least likely to visit; which eliminated southern California, Florida, and Hawaii from his list of possibilities.

Jeremy left the building to a setting sun as he walked back across campus to the library. The sun highlighted the remaining patches of snow at the mountain tops to the east. The campus library was situated in the middle of the campus, as though reinforcing the idea that knowledge, studying, and dusty tomes were the most important aspects of life. As if to exploit this mantra, this university was one of the few in the nation to have a building entirely dedicated as a testing center for the university. Thousands of students entered the library and testing center each day, more than any other building on campus. Most students seemed to only appear in the open when they had to walk the dreaded steps from the library to the testing center.

Jeremy, grudgingly, had some studying that he needed to finish before returning to his apartment where his friends would only distract him. His only consolation, as he entered the glass atrium of the massive library, was that he did not need to take any exams for a few weeks. He wove his way through the last rush of students that were running for a quick bite from a vending machine in the nearby buildings. He skirted around some students who had been caught smuggling in a pizza and chips for a group study session.

There were a few locations in the library that Jeremy always selected when he was trying to study. There were floors that seemed to be the least used by other students. Jeremy suspected it was largely laziness in others that made them choose floors two through four. The third floor of the library, confusingly enough for freshman, was at the ground level with two floors above and beneath the main level. The second floor was easy to reach without having to exert too much energy. Gravity appeared to be stronger in the glass atrium, as it pulled numerous students down the stairs to the rich wood tables that stretched out under the walks, flower beds, and lawns above. The third floor did not have as many tables, but it had easy access the computer section near the main entrance of the building, allowing for a quick sidetrack to print off an assignment. In recent years, this section became the one area of noise for the library, as groups congregated for projects. The fourth floor of the library was fairly popular, because it housed more computers and televisions with VCRs and DVDs, for viewing video assignments for various classes.

For those more willing to walk further, there was always the fifth floor of the library. Not as many students found their way here; the students who enjoyed sunshine and a view of campus frequented this floor. Jeremy did not usually come up to the fifth floor, because it was still just too busy for him. He had always preferred the corner seat of classrooms and finding a quiet section of the library in which to study. He especially preferred these locations in case he ever got tired. He could sleep at a desk cube that was tucked away without the fear of disturbing others. Sometimes, if he was really exhausted, he would venture to lie down on the ground under the desk for a few minutes to stretch out.

For these reasons, Jeremy preferred the absolute lowest floor of the library. There were only a few sections of the first floor that were used with any amount of regularity by other students. Most of the floor was taken by some auditoriums and special collections. There was a section devoted entirely to what Jeremy thought were Human Studies. This section was used mainly by the students in the teaching, counseling, or health programs of the university. Located at the far south of the building were the arrays of group tables and business books, where most of the accounting and management students congregated. Jeremy found it easy to avoid them, because they always remained in their elite associations.

In the farthest corner, with the most outdate books; cubed desks lined the outside wall. Jeremy usually had the pick of the last three cubes; others rarely ventured this far into the library. Jeremy gravitated to this corner immediately on this afternoon. He loved these spots, because he could not see outside. While he loved the spring and summer months, being able to see outside would make it harder for him to focus. Jeremy would often lose track of time from secluding himself far underground in the library.

Jeremy laid out his books and notebooks on the desk and unpacked his small laptop computer. This far from the main sections of the library, and so far below ground, he was lucky to get a wireless signal; his occasional inability to connect to the Internet eliminated another possible distraction. Jeremy began studying for a test that he would have to take in a few weeks, but he found himself struggling even more with staying on track.

He always had problems focusing in the early spring. The smell of the first cutting of grass made him long for freedom from school and schedules. He loved the crunch of thawing grass and the smells of fresh life. He loved these things so much that if he sat in a building on campus that had a view of the outside, he would never accomplish anything. Jeremy was having an especially hard time focusing now that the baseball season had officially started.

Jeremy sat at the desk without being able to keep anything productive in his head. Within a few minutes, Jeremy was no longer looking at his computer. He had his hands behind his head and was leaning back with a contented smile on his face. Finally, giving in, he locked his computer screen; made sure the security lock would prevent anyone from walking off with his computer and left his desk.

Jeremy walked briskly to the north end of the floor in the Life Studies section of the library. Having always preferred working by himself when given the choice between that or a group, Jeremy had to avoid certain class members while he was in this section of the library. There was often someone from his classes to pester him into joining their group, thereby dividing their work into even smaller portions. Jeremy had too many projects flop to be suckered into another doomed group. He developed the skill of skirting around the edges of this section of the library and ducking in to the aisles that were nearly never used by future sociologist majors.

Jeremy no longer had to look at the markers on the shelf ends to find the aisle he sought. Likewise, he did not need to spend very long finding the books he wanted to explore. Jeremy pulled down a selection of books to create a small pile by him as he sat down to lean against the opposing shelf.

At the entrance of the library, Jeremy's closest friends, Judy and Steve, were wandering in to find him. With a few words of whispering, Steve was willing to follow Judy's lead to find Jeremy. Judy led them down the south end of the first floor of the library. While Steve continued to look lost, Judy was able to find the desk where Jeremy had left his work and belongings.

"Well, where is he?" Steve asked.

"I think I have an idea," Judy said with a sigh.

"Okay detective," he said sitting down in the chair, "sleuth away."

"Get up off your butt and follow me," Judy said softly as she walked away. Steve groaned as he followed her out.

Steve was a conglomeration of football stereotypes. He had the shoulders of a middle linebacker, the legs of a kicker, and self-confident smile of a wide receiver. He kept his brown hair cropped short, exposing his domineering brow. His left ear displayed the traces of being mangled and scarred from cauliflower ear, as a result of full contact sports in high school. Steve followed Judy like a lumbering bear on the prowl. Steve was not large in stature as much as he was large in presence. Anyone who did not know him would think his humor was sparse and is attitude sour. Judy and Jeremy had learned that he was, in fact, harmless.

Steve followed Judy's lead throughout the library, trying to hide his admiration for her form. She was not tall or short. She walked with the grace of a potential ballroom dancer. Judy rarely wore shorts when the weather warmed; her well-to-do parents had raised her to favor skirts. Much to the annoyance of many other female students, Judy could wear a skirt in almost any weather and attract the eye of not a few males. Judy's over-the-shoulder-length brown hair carried a natural wave that required little instruction or preparation and complimented her face and frame. She did not need to wear very much makeup; her bright eyes, slight upturned nose, and full lips around a white smile did enough to draw attention to her. Judy smiled at nearly everyone she saw on campus, and Steve could never understand how she was so happy when she went to classes. She stood tall despite her school bag defying the laws of physics with the amount it could hold for her various classes.

Jeremy was completely lost into the stack of books around him when Judy and Steve snuck up on him.

"Hi!" Judy said as she sat down quickly and neatly on the stack of books, tucking her ankles behind her.

"Judy!" Jeremy said in a loud whisper. "What are you doing here?"

"Visiting you," Steve said as he lay down across the laps of Judy and Jeremy with his head in Judy's lap, scattering the books. "What does it look like we're doing?"

"Well, it looks like you are trying to distract me more than anything else," Jeremy grunted under the added weight while extraditing a book from under Steve thigh.

"Well, that is what I'm doing," Steve said with a satisfied smile, "but I have no idea what Judy is doing here."

"Quiet you two," Jeremy hissed while Judy and Steve chuckled. "This is a library."

"Oh, is that what this building is?" Steve said in wonder. "I think this is my first time in this building."

Muttering to himself Jeremy said, "You know, I would not even be surprised if that was true."

"So, what are you doing and why aren't you at your usual spot?" Judy asked Jeremy.

"I was studying," Jeremy whispered through the effort of shoving Steve off of their laps. "But then I got bored very quickly and came over here to look up some stuff about baseball."

"Haven't you had enough baseball for one day?" asked Judy as she looked through the titles on which she had been seated.

"You can never have enough baseball," Jeremy mumbled through his book.

"But, what else would you want to know?" Steve asked through a yawn. "I think these dusty, molded things are making me sleepy."

"They are called books," Judy said testily as she completed the task of removing Steve from their laps.

Jeremy did not answer them as he picked up the other books to replace them back on the shelf. He continued to ignore their conversation as they followed him back to his belongings. However, neither Steve nor Judy seemed to notice that Jeremy was lost in his thoughts as they left the library.

-THREE-

A few days later, Jeremy was sound asleep in the bed of his basement apartment. He did not have to think for long that the day was going to be another day that he'd rather spend entirely asleep. Giving into sleep, Jeremy promptly turned off the alarm before it could continue to disturb him. Even though his window was south-facing and exposed to the sun, there were enough trees and other apartment buildings to shield the majority of the sun light throughout the day.

Jeremy was not able to enjoy a day of sleep, because within five minutes, his roommate's alarm went off. Soon after, his other roommates would be banging about with cereal bowls from the kitchen on the other side of the bedroom wall at Jeremy's head. Jeremy knew that he had been defeated in his attempts to have a personal sick day from classes. Not wanting to get too far behind in his daily routines, Jeremy slumped out of the bed and went off to shower.

His shower did not entirely wake him up for the day. Neither did any of his other routines of eating a bowl of oatmeal and an English muffin while checking his email, RSS feeds, and Twitter updates from authors, sports teams, and companies. At an hour after his alarm went off, Jeremy grabbed his books and bag, gave one last longing look to his bed, and left the apartment for class.

His day passed by the same as most of the days he had class. Jeremy spent class after class studiously taking notes, without any variation or awareness of what was being taught. Occasionally, he would have a class with Judy or Steve. Steve was usually just as bored as Jeremy, while Judy tried to keep a positive outlook. On most days of the week, Jeremy had two hours between his morning and afternoon classes to spend his time eating and studying outside, now that the weather was beginning to consistently stay warm. On the days when Judy and Steve were able to accompany him, Steve would doze while he was listening to music in his headphones. Judy usually remained quiet as she studied or wrote furiously in her notebook. Jeremy was content with this little circle. They knew how to enjoy their time together as friends while still getting their work done for their classes. The majority of their days together were spent in almost complete silence. The three of them seemed to liven–up a bit after dinner for the few remaining hours of the day, before trying to get some sleep for the routine to start all over again in the morning.

Jeremy left Judy and Steve to head off to his last class of the day. He usually arrived early so that he could grab a snack from one of the vending machines in the lobby of the building. Today, he was unfortunate, finding that all of his favorite snacks had evaporated from the machines. He slumped into class with his stomach growling and texted Judy and Steve to bring something by his class as soon as possible. Jeremy was not surprised when Steve texted his refusal and smiled when Judy said she would bring by something healthier than vending-machine food for him.

By the end of class, Jeremy no longer felt hungry, due to the fruit smoothie Judy had snuck to him during class. Jeremy daydreamed about what favor Judy would exchange for the smoothie as he walked in a brisk pace back to his apartment, glad to be done with classes for the day. He settled on the idea that Judy would either have him accompany her to dinner, go for a hike, or iron her skirts as compensation.

Once inside his apartment, he went to the extra room in the apartment. His apartment could accommodate six renters, though they currently had five. The extra bed lay bare on the frame; unused by anyone other than Jeremy. He left his bag in the front room of the apartment while he awkwardly relocated the spare mattress out into the hall. After securing the mattress vertically against the wall of the adjoining room, Jeremy taped a rectangle with duct tape where he'd approximate a strike zone would be located. He dashed back inside his room to grab his glove and ball and returned to his makeshift practice lane.

The room Jeremy used in the basement was rarely used by anyone else in the building. If anything it was used late at night by a drummer and guitarist who thought they demonstrated extreme talent, despite the numerous complaints to the contrary.

Jeremy set the timer on his watch, began stretching his right shoulder, and walked to the farthest end of the room that still gave him space for a wind up. Then, with a final shake of his arm, Jeremy started pitching against the mattress.

Immediately Jeremy was somewhere else in his mind. He was no longer focusing on being in the musty basement of the apartment. Instead of pitching against a mattress, he envisioned he was at a diamond by himself. He struggled to imagine that he was pitching the full distance from a pitcher's mound. Jeremy tried to let his mind relax from focusing on the pain in his shoulder.

He let his mind drift into what he had read a few days ago about pitching technique. Jeremy tried to recall every picture and instruction, how to grip the ball, proper windup motions, and when to release the ball. Soon, he was not even focusing on what he had read.

His mind tended to wander when he got into a rhythmic routine, maintaining enough focus to think about his arm and the release. As much as possible, Jeremy sought a calm center as he pitched. As much as possible translated to hardly ever, because the pain in his arm would begin to scream at him.

Accompanying the pain were doubts and frustrations. He had never played organized baseball growing up and had focused on other sports. His right, and throwing, shoulder had been dislocated six times in high school wrestling. Another injury in wrestling made his lower back spasm in protest whenever he overexerted his pitching or lifting. Now, the unchecked injuries kept him from learning something he wished he had learned before.

As he packed the mattress back into his apartment, Jeremy continued down the mental path of disappointment and embarrassment. He never had an interest in baseball when he was younger. By the time he was in high school, he was involved in other sports, but he began to enjoy watching the game. Now he wished he had learned how to play baseball when he had the chance. There was only so much he could do to learn about the rules of the game. The remorse he felt was the remorse of missed opportunity. Now that he wanted to get into the game, he did not have all of the tools for training. He did not have access to a trainer or a coach. He knew that the closest he could come to reaching his dream of playing baseball were the pickup games on random weekends and the intramural college leagues through the late spring and early summer.

Jeremy left his apartment to walk across campus again, to head over to the college athletic facilities for the open use times. In the late afternoons to early evenings of the week, specific facilities were opened for use by the general student body. The facilities had a number of racquet ball courts, basketball and volleyball courts, numerous weight rooms, an indoor track, dance halls, two lap pools, and a diving pool. Of all of the facilities, Jeremy occasionally used the weight rooms, but he spent most of his time in the lap pools.

All of Jeremy's physical exercise was based on what he had done in high school or routines he could find on the Internet. He began swimming when he came to college after reading about the therapeutic benefits on sports injuries. His knees were shot from running in high school, and his shoulders hurt even when he woke up each morning. Swimming gave him the cardio workout, while also keeping his shoulders and back loose, and reduced the degree of pain after workouts.

When Jeremy finished the last lap in the pool, he slowly climbed out to the bench where he left his towel. Letting the cool air dry him off as he sat on the bench, Jeremy leaned his tired body against the tile walls. He pulled off the goggles and peeked at the clock on the wall to see how late his workout had kept him. Through the windows above the clock, Jeremy saw a familiar person waving to get his attention. Judy pointed towards the south of the building and Jeremy nodded. She left the windows and Jeremy went off to shower.

When Jeremy got out to the lobby, which Judy had been referring to with her waves, he found her sitting on a couch reading. Jeremy slumped on the couch next to her with a groan.

"Good swim?" Judy asked.

Jeremy let out another groan in protest of being required to speak.

"Do you have any homework?" Judy asked with a smile.

"No, why?" Jeremy mumbled.

"Good, I do," she said joyfully. "You can help me with mine," she said as she packed her book into her bag and left the couch. Jeremy grumbled as he went to catch up with her on the way out of the building.

As they made their way back to the campus library, the sun was behind the western mountains, leaving a mix of purples, reds, and oranges through the sky at their backs. Judy always refused to study in Jeremy's locations, insisting that he was being "anti-social" in those spots. Jeremy never won any of their arguments that in a library, you were not supposed to be social.

As usual, Judy led Jeremy to one of the upper floors of the library. The sun-loving crowds on these levels seemed too thin in the evenings, because there was no longer any sunlight to stream through the windows. The basement floors always seemed to be packed with students during the night. Jeremy speculated that this was due to the fact that they, like him, had finally reached a point of necessity, to not acknowledge the time of day and, instead, become immersed in the ever-increasing enslavement of midterm exams.

Judy spread her work out across a table and nodded that Jeremy should sit on the other side of the table. Jeremy pouted into his seat and waited for Judy's instructions. "What am I going to do to help?" Jeremy asked.

"You are going to proofread my essay while I study for another class," Judy smiled without looking at him.

"Yay, I'm so thrilled," Jeremy said in an undertone.

Judy slid across her essay, handed a pen to Jeremy and sat down to study. Jeremy struggled to stay awake after swimming. His eyes felt so heavy, and he could not keep his head up straight to focus on the writing. Judy giggled every time that his head drooped so far that his nose brushed the surface of the desk, which startled him awake.

After an hour of fighting off sleep, Judy tossed a wadded ball of paper at Jeremy, who had given up and laid his head down over crossed arms. Jumping in his seat, Jeremy looked wildly around the library for the source of disturbance. Judy failed to stifle a laugh that prompted glares from the other nearby occupants of the library.

Jeremy noticed the ball of paper and opened it expecting to see a note inscribed inside. He looked up lamely at Judy when he was met with a completely blank piece of paper.

Smiling, Judy leaned across the table, tucked her brown tresses behind an ear and whispered, "Want to go watch a movie instead of working?"

"Absolutely," Jeremy said relieved.

Jeremy helped Judy pack up her belongings before heading back down to the main floor of the library. Jeremy's spirits fell, however, when they stepped out of the library to be met with a heavy rain.

"I hate rain," Jeremy mumbled as he opened the spare umbrella Judy handed him. "Always calls off games."

"But there was not a game tonight," Judy said.

"I know, but if there had been a game, it would have probably been called off by the look of this storm," Jeremy griped.

"It's just a game. They always reschedule," Judy said opening her own umbrella.

"It's not just a game," Jeremy huffed, "It is Ameri…"

"America's Favorite Pastime," Judy finished sarcastically.

"Exactly," Jeremy said, choosing to ignore her sarcasm as they walked in the direction of their apartments, "and I need baseball as often as I can get it."

"So, we'll watch a baseball movie," Judy suggested.

"Really?" Jeremy said shocked at her willingness.

"No, not really," Judy said walking ahead of him. "I get to choose the movie tonight."

"Gee, sounds like fun," Jeremy stomped in a puddle which missed Judy and only soaked his legs more. "This night just gets better and better."

"It will be fun. You know you like my taste in movies."

"Only because they usually lull me to sleep in under five minutes," Jeremy shot back.

Judy retaliated by shaking her umbrella in his face before running ahead laughing.

-FOUR-

Judy and Jeremy enjoyed a friendship free of worry or concern. They felt like they could spend much of their day together, without anyone else, and not feel awkward. Jeremy never entertained the notion that he and Judy were anything other than extremely good friends. He never dared to try to clarify this with Judy for two reasons. First, he hoped she felt the same way, and second, he was slightly worried that such a conversation would introduce an awkward tension into their friendship.

Most of their time together was not spent in conversation. They studied together and helped each other with errands. By all means, they had the makings of becoming a boring couple; according to Steve's definitions of couple-hood. The friendship they shared did come with a share of compromises.

One early Saturday morning, a week later, Jeremy had to pay a portion of that price when his phone woke him earlier than he appreciated. He turned off the alarm on his phone, rolled over to go back to sleep, and instantly understood why Judy had been interested in his phone the night before. Minutes later there was a sharp rapping at his window.

Someone was clearly moving the bushes away from the window allowing more sunlight to filter through the blinds. The persistent knocking continued at the window, and Jeremy's roommate began to groan in protest. Jeremy pulled open the blinds to see a smiling Judy in his window, haloed by the early light. The morning was not as bright as he had thought. Jeremy was surprised at just how much shade the bushes provided. He could not stay interested for long as Judy's smile turned to a scowl.

"Come on sleepy head," Judy's muffled voice came through the glass.

"I don't believe this," Jeremy groaned, starting to close the blinds on Judy.

"Jeremiah Chase, you promised," Judy scolded through the glass.

"Are you insane?" Jeremy whined, "I would never promise to wake up at this time!"

"Dude, shut up!" groaned Jeremy's roommate.

"Jeremy, you get your butt out here," Judy commanded while pressing a finger to the glass.

Jeremy mumbled his sarcastic consent as he closed the blinds before falling back into his bed. Moments later his phone sounded again, though not as the alarm clock. Jeremy did not need to look at the phone to know that Judy was calling him to make sure he could not fall back asleep. He answered the phone just long enough the mutter an "I'm up," before snapping it shut.

After sliding out of bed, Jeremy quickly dressed, grabbed some water and snacks, and stuffed them into his hiking pack. When he met Judy waiting for him outside he was trying to extricate a banana from his pack.

"This is going to be so much fun," Judy said jumping to her feet.

"Yeah, loads," Jeremy said sarcastically. Judy responded by throwing a granola bar at Jeremy. "Ouch," he groused when the granola bar collided with his nose.

"Quit complaining," Judy said, turning away from Jeremy and walking to her car. "This was partly your idea."

"Yeah, which part? Definitely not the early morning part," Jeremy yawned while rubbing his nose.

Jeremy climbed into the passenger seat of Judy's car as she started the engine. She directed the car towards the mountains and wove through the still-sleeping neighborhoods. The drive lasted just short of a quarter of an hour; which was just enough time for Jeremy to fall back to sleep. Judy parked the car at the base of a trail that led up the mountain. The path was broad and manufactured. The ascent was steep and mostly unpleasant. The trail had never been very beautiful this low on the mountain face and so close to campus. The vegetation was just returning after a horrible prank resulted in a fire that spread across most of the face of the mountain five years earlier.

In the mornings of spring, Judy often wished to accompany the birds in the budding-growth of the mountain. Jeremy knew, however, that they would not be so fortunate in this area. Though the path was without natural beauty, the route was frequented by man throughout the year. The trail ended at a large cement landing on the face of the mountain. Many would ascend to the outcropping and look down at campus below them. The trail was only about two miles long. The steepness of the mountain gave the illusion of greater distance. On quiet, midday hikes in the previous semester, Jeremy and Judy were convinced they had heard the bells on campus from the landing on the mountain.

Jeremy and Judy huffed in silence as they made the journey to the top. Judy had insisted on a morning excursion, because there would not be as many hikers to disturb the tranquility of a sunrise on the mountain. They once made the mistake hiking the mountain in the afternoons and were annoyed to find couples trying to make out on the platform or set off dry ice bombs. This morning, the platform was empty. Judy led Jeremy to sit on the side of the platform with their legs hanging off the edge.

"Ah, this is nice," Judy said as she settled onto the platform next to Jeremy. She accepted some breakfast bars and a bottle of water as a reward for the hike. "Nothing like an early morning hike when it is still slightly chilly and waiting for the morning sun to warm us; right Jeremy?"

"Except for actually sleeping in just once on a Saturday?" Jeremy squinted under his hat to her. "Though I'm not even sure if I know what the term 'sleeping in' really means anymore."

Shoving Jeremy in response, Judy said, "Wow, look who woke up on the wrong side of the bed this morning."

"Nothing to do with the wrong side, Judy," he said through a mouthful of granola. "It has everything," he swallowed, "to do with waking up. It is quite the painful process."

"You are truly pathetic. Why do I spend any time with you?"

"I don't know. Animal Magnetism," Jeremy said wryly.

"Um, no, definitely not," Judy corrected seriously. "It's because you make me feel better about myself."

"Really?" Jeremy asked surprised.

"Yep, how can I not when I am around someone so despicable," Judy smiled.

"Gee, thanks Judy," grumbled Jeremy.

"Oh, don't be so sour," Judy scolded. "You know I'm only joking."

Jeremy pointed a finger at her, "Truth in every jest. Truth in every jest, Judy."

"Whatever, grumps," Judy said turning to look down the valley. "Just enjoy the scenery while the sun rises."

Jeremy and Judy remained mostly quiet as they sat on the mountain. The sun took nearly an hour to rise over the peak. It was another half hour before any warmth could be gained from the rays. Shortly afterwards, Jeremy and Judy began their descent back down the mountain. Their progress was slower descending than ascending, from the loose footing. There were just enough loose rocks that Judy often clung to Jeremy's arm for support.

Jeremy hated walking downhill on steep trails. His knees ached with each step, and he had a phobia of falling down the trail. He would spend most of his descent envisioning his body tumbling down the mountain and meeting every conceivable rock and splintered branch. Judy kept scolding him for going down the mountain too fast. He feared that if he went too slowly, his legs would shake too much and he'd collapse. He told none of this to Judy and only grunted in response to her scolding.

They finished off the rest of the fruit and granola when they reached the car and washed it down with the rest of their water. Having their fill of breakfast, Judy drove them back to their apartments.

Jeremy did not enter his own apartment but took the opportunity to wash and clean his own car for the rest of the morning. By the time he had finished and put the cleaning supplies away, it was nearing the middle of the day, and Jeremy was beginning to get hungry again. However, he knew that he could not bring himself to eat without a good shower.

Jeremy entered his apartment, knowing that his roommates had left while he was cleaning his car, and was surprised to hear the television from the kitchen. Steve was sitting on the couch when Jeremy walked into the kitchen to get some water.

"About time you get home from where ever you ran off to," Steve called without moving to look at Jeremy. "I swear you and Judy are dating each other and trying to keep it a secret."

Jeremy responded by flicking the remains of his glass of water at Steve.

"Hey man!" Steve protested.

"You know better than to joke about that," Jeremy scolded. "We're just friends and nothing else."

"Alright, jeeze," Steve whined, using a blanket from the couch to dry himself.

Jeremy left Steve to go shower. Half an hour later, Jeremy came out of the bathroom with the towel around his waist. Steve was still watching television but had now spread out across the entire couch.

Jeremy opened a frozen pizza from the freezer and threw it into the oven. He went to dress while the pizza baked. By the time he had dressed and returned to the kitchen, the pizza's smell was starting to fill the room.

"Smells good," commented Steve.

"So, you really hang out with me just for my food," Jeremy accused in a joking tone.

"Yep," Steve said putting in a movie into the DVD player.

"Then why didn't you fix something for yourself?" asked Jeremy.

"And have to move? Nope, quite comfortable right here thanks," Steve admitted.

"Nice dude. Is there anything else I can get you highness?" sneered Jeremy.

"Hey, just remember you mooched off of me for two months."

Jeremy admitted, "That is true, but you are still not getting any of my pizza."

"Eh, no loss. I already had one before you got home."

Jeremy shook his head as he pulled the finished pizza from the oven. Jeremy sat at the table and ate the pizza slowly, watching the movie Steve had selected. The movie was one that both Jeremy and Steve knew well. Neither paid close attention; it became something to fill the silence. Steve would occasionally pull out his phone to respond to a text message. Jeremy let his mind drift in and out of focus; the movie entertained no one.

Finally, toward the end of the movie, Jeremy spoke, "Want to play catch before tonight's game?"

"Wanna play catch?" Steve teased. "I haven't played catch since I was a kid!"

"What are you talking about?" Jeremy asked, confused. "We threw around a couple of days ago."

"I know that, but it sounds childish when you call it catch," Steve explained.

"Whatever, you knew what I meant," Jeremy huffed.

"Sure, let's throw a bit before the game," Steve smiled.

Jeremy and Steve left the apartment after they grabbed two gloves from Jeremy's collection. They went out to the grass between the various buildings of the apartment complex.

Steve, after examining the glove in his hand, complained, "Why do you always give me the crappy glove?"

"Crappy? What are you talking about?" Jeremy questioned fiercely. "That glove is seasoned," he said while tossing the ball into the newer mitt.

"Seasoned?" Steve doubted. "You call this seasoned? It doesn't even close very well."

"At least it does that much," Jeremy laughed. "Besides, I'm more important, so I get the nice glove."

Mumbling to himself, Steve complained, "More important or the only one who feels he needs to own more than one glove?"

"Start running," Jeremy responded.

They started throwing back and forth across the grass as they gradually increased the distance between themselves.

"Ouch!" Steve called, shaking his gloved hand. "Dude! Not so dang hard!"

"It wasn't hard!" Jeremy said in defense, "You've thrown your share of stingers."

"Yeah? But, those last few stung more than most."

"Yeah? Well, you have never gone up against my pitching," Jeremy reminded.

"Bring it on if you think you can," Steve challenged.

"You think you can handle playing catcher?" questioned Jeremy.

"I'll be fine," Steve grumbled while getting into a crouch.

Jeremy paced the approximate distance to be a pitcher and began to wind up.

"Okay, now I'm getting nervous about this," Steve whined. "Can't I get some padding?"

"Just trust me," Jeremy said. He delivered a strike which made Steve yelp in pain and fright after catching the pitch.

"Okay! Okay! I believe you. You can pitch a lot harder than just throwing around," Steve said through his pain dance, shaking his hand. "Way too fast and hard for me to sit there unguarded."

"Just trust me, you sissy," Jeremy goaded. "I'll stay in a tight-enough strike zone. Just don't move."

Crumbling, Steve crouched again, "Yeah, with my luck the next one will be wild."

Jeremy began to clear his mind before starting another wind up. He needed to focus even more in order to keep Steve safe from any wild pitching. He delivered a number of strikes before he threw wild and winced in pain. Luckily, the pitch sailed six feet from Steve, who still flinched in fear.

"You alright?" Steve asked when he saw Jeremy clutching his shoulder.

"Yeah, it's nothing," Jeremy said through gritted teeth.

"Nothing?" Steve didn't believe him. "Man, when are you going to get that checked?"

"When it stops hurting," mumbled Jeremy.

"Yeah, because that makes sense," Steve said while his cell phone began to ring. "Hey, it's your girlfriend."

"My what?" Jeremy asked.

"Hey Judy," Steve answered into the phone.

"Not my girlfriend," Jeremy corrected while shaking his head and taking the glove from Steve.

"Yes, this is Jeremy's answering service," Steve continued. "We are headed to the game right now. Meet you there?" He paused for her response. "Okay. Well, I will tell your boyfriend. See you later," he said before hanging up.

"Such a jerk," Jeremy said, though he could have sworn that he could hear Judy shouting into the phone while Steve hung up on her.

"What did I do now?" Steve asked in a smile.

"She's not my girlfriend," Jeremy hissed.

"Sure she is! She's a girl and she's your friend," Steve said, as though teaching a child that one plus one equals two. "Therefore, girlfriend!" he said while throwing his arms in the air.

"You know that is not what you were talking about," Jeremy said as he removed the window screen from the window behind a bush right above his bed before tossing in the gloves and ball.

"You're right. I think she loves you," Steve said as Jeremy replaced the screen.

"Stop, please," Jeremy said, brushing off his hands. "Let's not talk about that, because one, it's not true, and two," he said ticking them off on his fingers, "because continuing this conversation will only make things complicated between the three of us."

"Hmm, interesting," Steve said as he looked at his phone and started walking to the game.

-FIVE-

Because they were at a parochial institution, Jeremy, Steve and Judy were required to attend church services regularly each week. Most of the single students at the university would attend services in groups at the various locations around campus. Steve tended to have a rather unique view of the purpose of attending worship services.

"Hey, pretty boy," Steve announced as he let himself into Jeremy's apartment one Sunday morning. "Are you ready?"

"Nearly there," grunted Jeremy in response to the snide question.

"It's not like you need to impress Judy," Steve said glancing through the bathroom door to join his reflection with Jeremy's. "You've already won her over."

"I'm serious," Jeremy bit, "Drop it," he said growing even more frustrated at these remarks and the awkwardness it brought into their friendship with Judy.

"Okay, okay," Steve said. "Just hurry up or we're going to be late."

"And you care so much because?" Jeremy asked through putting toothpaste on his toothbrush.

"Church honeys. All about the Church honeys," Steve responded smugly and without a moment's hesitation.

Jeremy paused and stared at his friend in the mirror, "thath tho wong on tho mame lethels," he tried to scold through the toothpaste while Steve laughed his way into the kitchen for a second breakfast.

Jeremy finished getting ready for the services by putting on a tie after he had spit out the toothpaste; a product of too many mistakes from his teenage years when he was trying to impress a girl at church. He gave his blazer a cursory once over to make sure there were no stains, wrinkles, hair, or other needs for dry cleaning, before slipping it around his shoulders.

"I'm not trying to impress anyone," he said to himself as his arms slowly slid through the blazer, creating static electricity through his shirt. "I just want to look presentable."

After a few more minutes Steve and Jeremy walked out to Judy's building. The sun was just starting to shine over the top of the mountains and bring with it some warmth to the valley. Judy and Jeremy lived in the same apartment complex with separate buildings for male and female apartments. Judy's apartment was across the courtyard from Jeremy's and on the second floor of her building. Steve knocked promptly on Judy's door before ramming his hands into his pockets. Judy came to the door and let herself out before turning around to lock the apartment door.

"So boys," she said while sliding the key out of the lock, "Who will be my escort today?"

"Jeremy," Steve said.

"Steve," Jeremy tried to say louder.

"Remember, church honeys," Steve said seriously, wagging a finger at Jeremy. "I can't be seen escorting another girl to church. I won't have a chance with the church honeys."

"What makes you think you have a chance with them?" Judy said distractedly while rummaging in her purse.

Steve swore at Judy's remark.

"Such appropriate language before church," Jeremy said opening the door of the complex to lead Steve and Judy out.

"Yeah, yeah," grumbled Steve.

Judy was laughing, "Come on, we are going to be late."

"If we're late, I blame twinkle toes here," Steve said thumbing to Jeremy.

"Unless we are late because you get struck down from Heaven while walking," Jeremy intoned.

"Come on boys," Judy said exasperatedly, stopping the argument. "One of you should be a suitable escort." She glanced quickly at their refusal to volunteer. "I guess that leaves you, since we can't ruin what little chance Steve has for attracting a female," she said, looping her arm through Jeremy's. Steve failed in his attempt to hide his laughter as a cough.

As they walked to church, Jeremy was uncomfortably aware of the pressure from Judy's arm. It wasn't painful, nor was he sure it was entirely pleasant. He worried about being too comfortable with her or with being too stiff in her presence. Occasionally, a light breeze would flutter the hem of her modest skirt around her tanned knees and upper calves. Jeremy couldn't help but notice this when he let her lead the way down steps as they made their way across campus to the chapel. He quickly caught himself and checked to see if Steve noticed; he never did.

Judy paused for Jeremy and Steve to catch up. As she turned her head, the breeze caught her hair, which whipped out and tickled Jeremy's nose. "Oops," she giggled, "Sorry about that." She tried to hold her arm out again for Jeremy to take, but he surreptitiously found his pockets more interesting. They finally reached the chapel with Steve leading the way; scanning the congregation for lonely church honeys. Jeremy led them to a pew toward the back and slipped in just before the services started.

Midway through the services, as Jeremy was starting to doze, Steve leaned across Judy and hissed, "Psst. What about that one?" Jeremy glanced at him, "Three rows up and four to the right," Steve pointed.

"Will you two pay attention!" Judy scolded between them.

"I am paying attention," Steve protested.

"To the sermon," Judy said visibly disgusted.

Looking at Jeremy, Steve said, "Your girlfriend is mean."

"We're not dating!" Judy and Jeremy whispered loudly together, causing others to glance at them quickly before turning back to the sermon, but with less attention towards the latter.

"Now be quiet and pay attention," Judy hissed at Steve, out of the corner of her mouth as her face turned a deeper red than her blouse.

"Yes ma'am," Steve consented as he slumped in his seat.

Jeremy briefly wondered at what had upset Judy more, that Steve was disturbing the sermon, checking out girls, or asking Jeremy for his opinion on the girls.

Steve never seemed to find "a lonely church honey" in need of his attention throughout the sermon or in the Sunday school instructions. Jeremy followed close to Judy and Steve as they navigated the crowd at the end of the meetings on their way out of the door. Steve impersonated a giraffe by stretching his head above the crowd to re-evaluate the few "potentials" he had found during the day.

The day was reaching its warmest temperature as they made their way up the hills back to their apartments. The warm season was still young enough to share a good amount of cooler breezes, teasing warm relief when the breeze died. Judy walked close to Jeremy as they walked. Jeremy kept himself distracted as Steve enumerated on the pros and cons of each girl he saw at church. Judy would occasionally, snidely, correct Steve's sexist assessments through clarifying questions. Jeremy wondered if Steve understood the real intent behind Judy's questions.

One of Jeremy's choice activities on a Sunday afternoon was to take long naps. His naps did not consist of a constant state of sleep, which would make it difficult for him to get a full night of sleep at the end of the day. Most of the time, a book would rest across his chest while his eyes began to drift close. Jeremy would let his mind wander through memories and day dreams while his eyes were closed, before finally drifting to sleep. At what felt like the exact moment that Jeremy was finally drifting into sleep, one of his roommates burst through his bedroom door to tell him that he had a visitor. Jeremy grumbled as he flopped off his bed and padded into the kitchen.

"Afternoon picnic time," Judy said as Jeremy blinked awake. "Steve, what do you want on your sandwich?"

Steve, who usually spent the afternoon watching sports in Jeremy's apartment instead of going to his own, looked up from the sports section of the newspaper and the television, "Oh, I'm not going."

"Why not?" Jeremy asked.

"We have enough for three grinders," Judy said, slicing bread.

"Thanks, but I'd rather be somewhere else," Steve said turning back to the sports.

"Rude," Judy huffed.

"Don't start that again," Jeremy warned Steve.

"I'll be hanging out with someone," Steve offered.

"Yeah?" Judy asked. "Who?"

"A girl from church," Steve smirked.

"When did you talk to her?" Judy asked.

"While Jeremy was asleep."

Jeremy said, "You got up from the couch?" and received a spinning sports section in response.

"I'm happy for Steve," Judy said, finishing her sandwich at the park.

"You should be worried for the girl," Jeremy said while wiping mustard from the corner of his mouth.

"Be nice Jeremy," Judy chided. "He might just be onto something."

"What do you mean?" Jeremy asked wary of the response.

Judy blushed and looked away from Jeremy. She stared away at the mountains while Jeremy vainly attempted to interpret what she meant so he repeated his question.

"Something that he said," Judy replied softly without turning to look at Jeremy. A reddish hue began creeping around the back of her neck. "About dating."

"What did he say?" Jeremy asked with a panic gripping his heart and lungs. He couldn't say that his heart skipped a beat; it seemed to seize up completely.

"Well, about us," Judy said lowering her head, but still not looking at Jeremy.

"Look," Jeremy swallowed, "I'm sure he's joking around. I know he can seem serious and I've tried talking to him," he rambled.

"I'm not so sure that he's joking around," Judy said, finally looking at Jeremy. "He seems to want to anchor himself a bit."

"What would he be doing it for if not to tease us?" Jeremy asked confused.

"Well," Judy started, "maybe he is testing our responses."

"Testing us why?" Jeremy asked. "Do you think he has feelings for you and wants to know if you are interested in him?"

"No, I don't think that is it either," Judy said. "I think he just wants some warning if we did get serious, so he wouldn't be left out or something."

"Left out?" Jeremy asked, trying to ignore Judy's if.

"Well, we are a little group. If you and I started dating, then he'd probably feel out of place, like he didn't belong."

Jeremy thought for a moment, "He could just find someone to date," and scared himself that instead of proposing a different idea, he had gone along with the hypothetical situation of dating Judy. Trying to recover, Jeremy said, "But, I still think that he's asking all the time, because he's interested in you." Jeremy decided it was time to let the conversation hang when Judy didn't respond. No matter how awkward it was to leave a break in the conversation, it would be more awkward if they continued talking about them dating.

That was until Jeremy let the pause hang for five minutes and realized that the pause could be construed to Judy as though he were considering the possibility of dating. Was she studying him and noticing the flush in his face? How would she interpret this silence or his facial expressions? He quickly knew that he had drastically made the wrong decision. Staying silent would certainly be construed in Judy's mind in ways that would mean trouble for Jeremy.

"It's getting late," Judy said so softly she was barely audible. "And a little chilly."

Jeremy sprang to clean up the remains of the picnic in an attempt to excuse his avoidance of making eye contact with Judy. The walk back to their apartments was awkward, and their conversation was disjointed. Jeremy had never known a time in their friendship when everything was so uncomfortable between them. His paranoid personality made him suddenly wish he could analyze everything he had ever said or done with Judy. He felt that he had to run damage control for appearing to be flirting with her, instead of just being a friend. Maybe he would have to spend more time just with Steve to compensate, but if he did that, then he would be isolating Judy, and then what signal would she be getting from him?

Judy had to say good night twice to Jeremy before he heard her. He finally started to understand what his father had always joked about; it's impossible to know what a woman is thinking just by looking at them.

-SIX-

Jeremy had a number of routines that he used to relieve stress or frustration. Most of the time these routines became a self-abusive cycle of exhaustion, because it was the only way to physically wear himself out before the anxiety took complete control of him and left him in a panicked mess. Whenever he felt particularly anxious, he would not want to walk across all of campus just to get out his frustration in a hard swim. Resorting to his alternative, Jeremy once again pulled out the spare mattress in the apartment and pitched out his frustration.

His relationship with Judy was becoming increasingly more complicated after their conversation at the park. He had enjoyed that they could spend so much time together without feeling awkward or having any thoughts of dating come up. Now, Jeremy wasn't sure that the idea of dating hadn't always been in Judy's mind. Their brief conversation filled Jeremy's mind like a fog. Now, it was all he could think about. In reality, Steve was right. It was easy to see that Jeremy's relationship with Judy was a very early stage of dating. They already spent so much time together but never showed any romantic feelings toward each other.

Jeremy kept pitching and imagined that he was throwing out any thought in his head about dating Judy. He could start to limit his time with her and try to be around Steve for more periods of the day. But, again, he knew that limiting his time with Judy would only increase the awkwardness between them.

Jeremy's cell phone rang, and, by the ring tone, he knew it was Judy. He ignored the ringing and threw harder; nearly throwing out his shoulder again. To answer, or not to answer; that was his question. Hating that not answering would only raise more distance Jeremy caught the call just before it went to his voice mail.

"Hi," they said over each other. "How are you?" Yep, thought Jeremy. Awkward.

"Um, has Steve returned from his date?" Judy asked.

"Not that I've seen, but he may just go back to his own apartment when it's over," Jeremy reminded.

"Oh yeah, I forgot." Judy said hurriedly. "I keep forgetting he actually lives in a different apartment."

"Define lives," Jeremy repeated their old inside joke.

"You don't think he'd come back to gloat about his date?" Judy asked.

"That does sound like him," Jeremy admitted. "But, he'll probably just compare it to us."

Silence. Great, Jeremy mentally kicked himself. Just the topic he wanted to avoid and he was the one who brought it up. "Well," Judy cut into his thoughts, "we'd just have to set him straight for the gazillionth time."

"Judy, I'm sorry if I," Jeremy started but was cut off.

"No, I brought it up in a weird way." Judy said.

"I just don't want you to feel like my reaction was…" he swallowed, "that I was turned off by you," Jeremy regretted saying the instant he finished. Again, he was the one to make it more awkward for them.

"So, what are you saying?" Judy said with a slight tease in her voice. "Do you want to start dating me?"

"No, I, um," spluttered Jeremy.

"Relax Jeremy," Judy laughed over the phone. "I don't want to date you."

"You don't?" Jeremy asked, not sure if he should be relieved or offended.

"I like just being friends and not having to worry about the whole dating thing," Judy explained.

"Yeah, me too." Jeremy said confused.

"Good," Judy said brightly. "I'm glad we cleared that up. Let me know if Steve shows up."

"Okay," Jeremy put in just before Judy hung up the phone. Too confused to pitch anymore, Jeremy put everything away and went off to bed.

-SEVEN-

Once the weekends began to be consistently warm, Jeremy and
Steve enjoyed the warmth with many other students by joining a
number of intra-mural teams. They were on the same teams if there
both played the same sport. Even though Jeremy did not like Ultimate Frisbee as much as Steve, they both played every Saturday
morning while the night cold was chased away by running students
as the sun lazed over the mountain top. Every other Saturday, de-
pending on the weather, they played in an intra-mural, co-ed, softball
league. They always tried to get Judy to play, but she always declined.

Jeremy never pitched for his team, because he wasn't comfortable
with his skill. It was easier to appear to be very knowledgeable about
the game of baseball when sitting in a stadium, especially when he
had access to the official rules in a small file on his phone. Out on
the field, however, he was not so confident. He enjoyed the game
about as much as the most experienced player, but, he wasn't confident enough to stand out. He hit and struck out just about as often
as everyone else. Just like when he was younger, Jeremy was the

average player. Steve was the only one on the team that knew Jeremy could really pitch. Steve was always volunteering Jeremy to pitch for the team, but Jeremy always refused and insisted on their normal pitchers. Jeremy kept trying to stop Steve, because this was just slow-pitch softball and not anything he was used to throwing.

Most of their games went without much incident. The only problems were with the student umpires; who Steve and Jeremy liked to heckle. Occasionally, they were stuck with one of the few umpires that knew even less about baseball than Judy. Even having never really played in an organized league, Jeremy still could tell where a strike zone was and what constituted as a bad call.

"Bad call ump!" Jeremy called at a sloppy toss that was called as the second strike for Steve.

"You want to call this game?" the short female field umpire yelled back; her face as red as her hair.

"No, that's what you are supposed to be doing!" yelled Jeremy, without pause.

The second baseman, who had been flirting with the female umpire all game, called out to Jeremy, "Her calls are fine. You just don't like the pitching."

"It clearly wasn't a strike," Jeremy retorted.

"Why don't you come out here and pitch then?" the pitcher yelled.

"Gladly," Jeremy said starting to walk out to the field.

"Get back to your bench or you are out of the game," the female umpire yelled while the umpire behind home tried to ignore that it was his calls that started the argument. He clearly felt that the female umpire could handle the situation.

Jeremy sat back down as Steve hit the third pitch but was thrown out at first. At the turn of the inning, the second baseman, still trying to defend the female umpire's honor, challenged Jeremy, "If you're such a hotshot, why don't you pitch this inning?" Jeremy's team looked at him and their pitcher, Sean, said he wouldn't mind taking a break.

"That's it," the second baseman from the other team said, stepping up to the plate. "Let's see how easy it is."

Steve, who played third base, called, "Jeremy, you know which pitch to use." Jeremy nodded and decided it would be worth the reprimand and the possible expulsion from the game. Winding up, Jeremy gave it his all and threw a hard strike as though trying out for the majors instead of playing a slow pitch softball game. The other team exploded, "Hey, its softball!" Jeremy's team hollered in delight. The umpires convened around Jeremy to threaten him with expulsion from intra-murals while Jeremy glanced around them to see the batter visibly shaken. Jeremy promised to behave and everyone started to calm down.

Trying to save face, the batter insisted on regular pitches instead of underhand. When the home-plate umpire agreed, hoping for a humbling experience for the batter so he'd stop hitting on the female umpire, Jeremy began his windup again. After the second strike, the other team began to quiet their cat calls, and Jeremy thought he heard Judy yell her support and tried to keep it out of his head. The last pitch was exactly like the first two; straight down the middle, a fast ball; he did not know how to throw anything else.

That night, Jeremy, Judy, and Steve were in the kitchen of Jeremy's apartment as Jeremy cooked dinner. Jeremy had only pitched against the one batter. No matter how much he enjoyed the display, he still wasn't comfortable in front of everyone and wasn't sure how long his arm would have lasted. Steve was still ranting about the umpires; despite the fact that they won the game. Judy was not really listening to Steve and simply trying to watch the TV around his pacing.

"Well, that should teach them to mouth off," Steve was saying about Jeremy's pitching.

"Especially since it was my mouthing off that started the whole incident," Jeremy said from the stove with is back to Judy and Steve.

"If they would just call the game right, none of this would have happened," Steve fumed.

Tired of the repeating conversation, Judy asked, "When is dinner?"

"About ten more minutes," Jeremy answered.

"I'm famished," Judy groaned and turned back to the TV.

"Wasn't he good?" Steve said proudly as he sat next to Judy.

"Yeah, he was," Judy said softly.

"Freaking awesome smack down," Steve said getting sucked into the TV.

"Word," Judy said with a mocking tone caught only by Jeremy, who silently chuckled as he finished preparing the dinner. "Dinner is ready," Jeremy announced over the television.

"Finally, food," Steve said with heavy emphasis.

"Mmmm. Smells good," Judy said, pouring the drinks.

"Let's hope it tastes good," Steve said with a grimace. "It kind of looks like barf."

"Gross," Judy said wrinkling her nose.

"It is beef stroganoff," Jeremy said, trying to remove any emotion in his voice. "I guess it does resemble regurgitated food."

"This doesn't look like any beef stroganoff I've ever had," Steve grumbled.

"Try it, it tastes good," Judy suggested.

"Or you could just leave and not have any," Jeremy offered and tried to ignore Judy's smile at this suggestion.

"Nope, too hungry," Steve said as he ate hurriedly. "Besides, I haven't told you my great idea."

"Does it involve pranks or girls?" Judy said into her plate.

Ignoring Judy, Steve said, "You should play for our college team. We all know the pitcher sucks. You can't be any worse than him."

"Except for the fact that I have no playing experience. I haven't been on a team since my one and only year in little league," Jeremy said, waving his fork. "And, I've got nothing special to offer."

"Sure, you can't play this year, but plenty of people walk on. You would blow them away with that arm."

"Oh, yeah. This arm will blow alright," Jeremy scoffed while dishing up some salad onto his plate. "My shoulder gets too tired and hurts too much for them to consider me. I won't be able to last long on this shoulder, even if I did strengthen it up."

"Why not throw with your left arm?" Judy asked. "You do just about everything else with either hand just as easily."

"Judy, you can't do that," Steve chided. "It's too hard to switch up like that. That's why practically no one does it."

"But, wouldn't that give him the edge he needs over the other pitchers?" Judy said seriously.

"It's not worth considering, because pitching with just one arm taxes your body too much. You have to specialize," Steve said. "No, not specialize, because no one has to choose what arm to use. They use the same arm they've always used. Jeremy's a freak."

"Thanks," Jeremy said in mock hurt.

"You are welcome," Steve said with finality.

"So, that's it?" Judy asked with a fork half raised to her mouth.

"It was a joke," Steve said. "You can tell just how fast they are pitching when you are sitting in the stands. You'd need more experience."

Although Jeremy was able to dodge the conversation of pitching for the rest of the evening, it had struck a cord with him. He'd always regretted not spending more time learning baseball when he was younger. Truth be told, Jeremy still had a lot to learn on strategy and technique, and he doubted he could ever learn that in a book.

Jeremy spent the rest of the night wondering if he could learn how to pitch with his left hand well enough to try out for the team. There were many situations where he had learned to use either hand to complete a task. Most of them were manual-labor skills but proved fruitful in many sports; why not baseball? The trouble was that he had never tried pitching with his left hand. He only knew one pitch with his right. It would undoubtedly be a difficult process to teach himself how to throw left handed. He would most likely find that pitching was one of those skills that would not translate well from right to left. Jeremy decided to push the day-dream from his mind.

-EIGHT-

A few days later, as Jeremy was walking in the morning to where he usually met Judy and Steve, he was still thinking about the possibility of learning how to pitch with his left arm. It could be just the edge he needed in a tryout, since he didn't have any other experience with playing in an organized league, or, was he simply desperate to be noticed for being able to do something different? He didn't focus much on what Steve was talking about as they met up on their way to meet Judy after her early morning class. Jeremy had brought along a box of powdered donuts, his favorite unhealthy breakfast.

"Good morning boys," Judy said cheerily, "What's new?"

"Nothing much," mumbled both Jeremy and Steve.

"Well, that's boring," Judy replied, snatching a powdered donut.

"What would you like to know?" asked Jeremy, smiling at the scandalized expression on Steve's face when one of their prized donuts was consumed by Judy.

"Well, since I had dinner with you last night, I doubt you have anything really thrilling to say," Judy said to Jeremy and turned to

Steve. "I only included you in the question out of courtesy. I really wanted to know how everything is with Steve and this mystery girl."

Failing to contain his laughter, Steve answered, "I do not kiss and tell Judy."

"You've kissed her already?" Judy asked incredulously. "That's a bit fast."

"Well, anything is faster than the speed you and Jeremy are going," Steve said helping himself to another donut.

Ignoring Steve, Judy said, "Well, if you won't tell us anything about your night, and I know Jeremy didn't say anything to you about our night, I will tell you while we walk to class."

"There is no way I want to hear about your make-out sessions," whined Steve.

"As much as we know you'd like a pointer, that is not what our relationship is like," Judy said, brushing powder off the corner of Jeremy's mouth.

"Steve, it really is getting old," Jeremy grumbled, trying to avoid Judy's gaze. "For your information, I made a big decision last night and it had nothing to do with dating Judy."

"But, you don't deny that you have thought of dating Judy!" roared Steve as though he finally got his friends to admit some secret.

"What decision did you come to?" Judy said over Steve.

"Well, I have mostly decided to try out as pitcher for next season," Jeremy said.

"I didn't think you had to try out for the intra-mural team," Judy asked with a smile.

"No, the college team," Jeremy said.

"You'll never make the team," Steve laughed. "You don't even have any experience. Even if you did, your arm would wear out too quickly."

"Which is why I'm going to learn how to pitch with my left as well," Jeremy said. "Maybe I'll stand out as something of value to the team if I can pitch with both arms. I'd be two pitchers in one."

"It's like I said before," Steve said, tossing the empty donut box in the trash. "They won't take you if you don't specialize on one arm. Why take a moderate pitcher that can throw with both arms over someone who can really pitch."

"Well, I think it's a good idea," Judy said.

"You would," Steve said to Judy. "You don't know baseball. The idea was a joke. Jeremy doesn't have much to offer anyone other than his freakish ability to do things with both hands equally well. Jeremy hardly knows baseball. Can you even throw anything other than a fastball?"

"I can learn," Jeremy said deflating. "I'd like to be able to say that I had tried instead of wasting a possible opportunity."

"Don't let him do this to you Jeremy," Judy said reddening. "If this is a dream of yours, then go for it. Desire will make up for experience."

"No it won't," spat Steve. "You're just being supportive, because you're waiting for Jeremy to get the stones to ask you out."

"That's not fair," Jeremy stopped short. "That has nothing to do with this. Not that she wants to date me. She's just being a supportive friend," he said, frightened at his own rising temper.

"Supportive?" said Steve. "Supportive doesn't mean you always have to agree with them. It means you stick with them through the hard times, but you should help them see reality."

"And why can't something as simple as Jeremy trying out for the team be a reality?" Judy asked.

"Look, it was just a silly thought. There's no need exploding about it," Jeremy said in an attempt to end the conversation.

"I'm not exploding," Steve said, trying to calm down. "I just hope you have thought this through."

"You sound like you don't want him to try at all," Judy accused.

"Look, freshman year I walked on in the football tryouts," Steve said. "I'd played football since little league. It's not easy. I thought I could handle it, if not out shine most. I was way out of my league." He waved off Judy's almost interruption. "I actually did make the team, but I wore out from being the practice for the starters. It's hard work, Jeremy. You don't have any experience. I've played baseball as well as football in high school, and can try to help you. We may be able to help you get up to tryout level with one arm. The pain in your shoulder may force you to stop before reaching tryouts."

"What's the difference with adding an additional arm? Wouldn't that help his odds?" Judy asked.

"Because he won't make it!" Steve yelled. "We need all this time to make him barely able to stand the rigorous tryouts for just one arm. We don't have the time for a foolish idea of adding another arm."

"If Jeremy thinks he can learn then let him try," said Judy.

"Hey, I said it was just a silly passing thought," Jeremy said. "I was just trying to change the subject from dating."

"Stop it Jeremy," Judy said. "Don't stop before you've even tried. Learn to pitch with your other hand. Anything can happen."

"I'll tell you what will happen," Steve said. "Either his arms will give out before he gets to tryouts, or he'll just make a fool of himself trying to tryout with both arms."

"Why are you so convinced that this cannot be done?" Judy asked.

"Why can't you two let this go?" Jeremy moaned unable to understand why they were so heated.

"Is it just because it's never been done?" Judy asked visibly ready to dispute this claim.

"Exactly and why haven't we heard about it being done? Because it's not reasonable. You think this idea was thought up for the first time in mankind by us? No, way. Not on your life," Steve said. "Someone has thought of it before and realized how stupid they would be to try."

Steve turned to Jeremy. "Maybe someone could pitch with both hands, but he clearly didn't amount to much or we'd all know his name.

"Jeremy, it's great to turn a dream into a reality. Just don't blow it by wasting time trying to learn how to pitch left handed on top of getting ready. It's not worth risking your only chance." Without another word, Steve turned and left Judy and Jeremy standing alone outside their class.

"I wasn't serious," Jeremy called after Steve. "Don't get so bent about me trying to change the subject."

Jeremy and Judy shared a table in their class. In the aftermath of Steve's irrational response, Jeremy was even more subdued in this class than normal. Even when they had to split into groups for an exercise, Jeremy hardly participated. He tried to ignore Judy's glances. She had been fuming when they entered the class, and he decided to let her cool off on her own. In his avoidance of her gaze, he didn't realize that she had calmed down and now only worried about him.

Jeremy could not understand why such a fleeting idea, when shared, resulted in such an argument. Being the psychology major, Judy would try to analyze Steve's reaction and explain Steve's reactions in a way that would only confuse Jeremy further. He had to admit that the thought of possibly trying out for the team was exciting; most of his daydreams were. Now, he wasn't sure that it was wise for him to have voiced the silly dream. Steve was right, he didn't have any experience. Jeremy's past sports injuries in his shoulders and back would most likely not be able to handle the strain. He should not have entertained the dream to the point of dreaming of one day pitching for the team.

Jeremy suddenly noticed the corner of notebook paper laying an inch from his hand. With the least amount of movement required to see the writing, Jeremy read.

I'm not even going to ask if you are okay. Try not to be mad at Steve. He just doesn't want to see you hurt. Don't give up! He read in Judy's handwriting, which filled the tiny corner in a neat yet hasty print.

At least she hadn't tried to psycho-analyze their friend, but maybe the analysis just could not fit on the corner of the page, and she was saving it for after class. Jeremy extended his fingers, hid the scrap in his hand and tried to make the most of the rest of the class. He found that he still could not focus. He couldn't explain why he was so consumed by what had happened between Judy and Steve. It was almost as though he wasn't really there in the argument. He had a sinking feeling that something lay at the core of the argument between Judy and Steve.

When their class let out, Judy and Jeremy left the building to follow their usual routine for the few hours before their next class.

"Are you hungry?" Judy asked, because their class was twice as long as most and ran to early lunch time.

"Not really, but I'll go with you if you are hungry," Jeremy said distractedly, navigating the bustle of students outside the various campus buildings.

"I'm not really hungry either," Judy said. "I'm just trying to get you to respond to something."

"I'm responding like normal Judy," Jeremy said as they ducked under an impromptu football toss that had migrated away from the grass and over the path.

"So, you'll stop avoiding me now?" Judy asked.

Jeremy didn't respond and just scowled deeper. His resolve to distance himself from Judy and not appear to be trying to date her had come at a horrible time.

"Why are you taking this so hard?" Judy asked.

"Because you both exploded on me and each other!" Jeremy said exasperated and unable to keep it inside him any longer. "You are supposed to be my friends. I felt like I had done something horribly wrong. I felt like I was on trial. I thought I was just sharing an idea and not having to diffuse a bomb or convince anyone. I wasn't even asking for support. Sure, I wanted feedback, but what the heck was that all about?"

"Why do you even need to convince anyone? Especially Steve? Why does his opinion really matter?" When Jeremy didn't answer she continued. "I know you consider him a great friend, but you are not trying to get him to try out for the team. You, Jeremy, not Steve, want to try out for the team." She said pushing her finger into his chest as though he had forgotten who he was. "I know you would like the support, but Steve isn't the only friend you have."

"Judy," Jeremy groaned, "it was a fleeting fancy. Not a dream. I don't really want to try out. Sure, it would be cool to play…"

"Don't try to trick me into thinking this isn't important to you," Judy cut in. "I know you've regretted not playing when you were younger. I know how much you live to watch the games, think about the sport, and dream about being in the game whenever we are watching one." Judy stopped and pulled Jeremy to face her. "Steve may give you a hard time or not believe in you. I'm still here trying to convince you to go through with this dream, and you're acting as though we've all turned against you. That hurts, Jeremy. It hurts that you don't value what I'm saying." Jeremy watched her storm away from him even more confused than before.

"Judy!" he called out too late to make a difference. "I wasn't being serious."

-NINE-

Jeremy couldn't focus on anything but the argument. His usual secluded spots in the library would offer no solace for his mind. He read uncomprehendingly while he replayed the argument in his head. He knew there was something right in front of him that his mind was refusing to see. Jeremy suspected it was the real reason behind why Steve and Judy acted the way they had. Everything about their reactions would be completely irrational without that one element. Jeremy was both curious and fearful of acknowledging that one factor, if he could figure it out. He knew Judy could identify it immediately in psychological terms, but he needed real-life answers and not an analysis. For once, he did not want to be analytical.

Jeremy's heart fell as his mind betrayed him and tried to analyze that morning. Could he have found himself in some childish triangle? He just wanted his two friends to accept each other, and him, for who they were.

A theory was becoming clear to him. Steve liked Judy and was jealous that Judy always favored Jeremy. Favored? It could only be that. Jeremy would not accept that she harbored any more intimate feelings for him than that. She had said on the night of their Sunday picnic that she didn't want to date Jeremy. He did not want to think about why she seemed to favor him over Steve. Jeremy had to believe that Judy suspected that Steve liked her but had not wanted to acknowledge this to Jeremy.

Accepting defeat in his attempts to study, Jeremy packed up his belongings and left the unforgiving library. As he passed the campus' student center, he saw a familiar person coming out one of the doors, throwing away the wrappings of a sub sandwich.

"Judy!" Jeremy called while trying to catch up. "Are you still mad at me?"

"No," she said unconvincingly.

"Then why did you brush me off?" Jeremy asked.

She spun at Jeremy, "Do I really have to spell it out? You can be so…" she threw her arms out in frustration. "You mope all morning and won't talk to me, but I'm the one who did something wrong by not wanting to talk to you."

"I know, you are right," Jeremy said softly. "I'm sorry," he said pulling out his wallet. "I want to show you something," and he pulled out a slip of paper.

"What is this?" Judy asked.

"It's the hours of the Athletic department. That's who I have to talk to first for trying out for the team. I picked it up between classes." Judy didn't look up at Jeremy, so he continued. "I figured it wouldn't hurt to at least go talk to them and find out if tryouts are even a possibility for me before I start training."

"Why are you showing me this?" Judy asked.

Jeremy was surprised at her vehemence, "I just thought…"

"Do you think this will make everything better?" she asked.

"I thought so," Jeremy said unsure. "You were right about how I was acting today, and I'm sorry."

"Don't do this for me, Jeremy. Don't do this to get back to good terms with me," she said sharply. "Apologize because you are sorry, that's fine, but don't go through with the tryouts because of me. Do this for yourself."

"I am," though he was not sure he was being honest with himself.

"And don't do it just to prove Steve wrong. There may be people who do not agree with your choices to pursue a dream. If you feel it is right, then you need to go for it. If they are proved wrong as a result, then so be it, but don't let that be your goal," she said looking deep into his eyes. "Don't prove your friend wrong. You need your friend."

"I thought you said Steve wasn't my only friend," he said, risking a smile.

"Yeah, well, the problem I had with you is fixed for now. Fix things with Steve, and just leave me out of everything," she said, turning away from him again.

"Fine," he said, lifting his shoulders. "Can I walk you home?"

"Thanks, but I need to do some stuff in the library tonight. I'll see you tomorrow," she said over her shoulder.

"Judy? Are we really okay?" Jeremy asked.

"Yeah, we are. Sorry I was so harsh earlier. I was being stupid."

"No, you were being honest," he said before thinking. It must have been the right thing to say because her shoulders relaxed. "Have fun studying Judy."

"See you tomorrow Jeremy," and she turned away to the library.

He was lying to himself. He had always been a day-dreamer. His entire life had been spent day-dreaming about the elusive "What if I" scenario. What had been a childish pastime was becoming a problem in college. Jeremy could not decide on a program, because he always changed his mind with new daydreams of life with each program.

Once he was back in his apartment, Jeremy resorted to his personal therapy again. As he set up the mattress in the common room, he seriously considered just leaving the mattress against the wall, even when he wasn't using it, just to save him the trouble of packing it in and out of his apartment.

Tonight was different for him; he started off by stretching his left arm as well as his right. He threw right handed twice, slowly, internally analyzing how he moved and translating the reverse movements for his left side.

Pitching from the left side is a horrible experience when you were only used to the right. Jeremy felt like he was forcing his body into having a seizure, as his left arm tried to throw the first pitch. It just plain hurt to throw left handed. He couldn't figure out how his feet should move or how to turn his body. Nothing had ever been this hard to learn with both hands. It was always easy for him to learn how to translate an action from left to right. Now, for the first time, Jeremy felt like he would have to create a completely new style of pitching for his left, instead of doing a straight mirror of the process.

Pitching would probably have to be the same situation for him. He would have to learn how to pitch as a completely different person. With his next pitch, Jeremy was able to catch his reflection in the front of the drum set that was always left in the room. His left arm just didn't look right as it arced through the pitch. It wasn't fluid like his right arm. Jeremy decided that he'd need to watch some slow videos of left handed pitchers to get some pointers, since he didn't have a pitching coach at his disposal. The only things that came to mind were a few favorite baseball movies where the pitcher was left handed. It wouldn't be the best resource, but it would hopefully be better than nothing.

Jeremy received an unexpected surprise the next morning, considering the events of the previous day. Steve was waiting outside Jeremy's apartment when he opened the door.

"Hey, ready to go?" Steve asked tentatively. When Jeremy didn't respond he continued, "What, thought I wouldn't show up?"

"Honestly, yeah I did," Jeremy admitted, locking his door.

"Yeah, about yesterday," Steve said. "I don't really know what to say."

"Honestly, what's the harm in just finding out if trying out is even possible? I just want to know," Jeremy cut in.

"Really, that's all?" Steve said skeptically.

"Well, no. If I can try out, then I am going to try," Jeremy said.

"Despite not having any real experience," Steve reminded again.

"Well, that's why I want to talk to the department and see if I can talk to the coach. I would rather find out if I will even be allowed to try out before I waste the time trying to train," Jeremy said.

"Judy would say that sounds like you are already preparing to not try hard enough," Steve said.

"Well, the way you two acted yesterday got me thinking," Jeremy admitted as they walked onto campus. "I'm still curious about how open the tryouts are."

"If they're nice, they will say go ahead and show up, but if they're honest…" Steve let the thought hang.

"They'll probably say that I shouldn't waste my time," Jeremy tried to chuckle.

"Well, I guess it never hurts to be prepared about what they'll say," Steve said.

"Exactly," Jeremy said glad that Steve had yet to explode on him. "What do I have to fear? I know the range of possible answers, so I might as well find out which answer it will be."

"You're really serious about this?" Steve asked. "It's not a fleeting thought like you were claiming yesterday?"

"I was just saying that because I was trying to get you two to calm down. Seriously, what was all of that?" admitted Jeremy.

"We support your dreams, just like we know you'd support ours,"

Steve said sharply. "Let's just leave it at that."

-TEN-

Later that day, Jeremy, Steve, and Judy fell back into the routine that had been interrupted by Jeremy's announcement the day before. They all met at a predetermined location on campus after their morning classes to share a few hours of break before they split for their individual schedules.

"Well, what's the plan?" Judy asked cheerily.

"I vote for food," Steve said, sounding more like his usual self.

"No surprises there," muttered Judy in an undertone. "What's your vote Jeremy?"

"I'm going to find out if I am allowed to try out for the baseball team for next year," Jeremy said.

"Wow, so soon?" Steve stiffened. "Shouldn't you think about this more?"

"I need to do this before I chicken out about asking." Jeremy caught the instance stiffness in Steve and Judy and how they averted their gazes from each other. "So, I guess I will catch up with you?" he asked, painfully aware that it was too soon to have brought up the topic with them again.

"Or, we could come with you," Judy offered.

"Okay, if you want," Jeremy said.

Steve acted distracted as he said "Sure," while miming rubbing his stomach in hunger.

"Don't worry, it should be a quick stop," Jeremy said. "So your food isn't too far away Steve."

They walked down the hill toward the athletic buildings in relative quiet. Jeremy tried not to talk, because there were only two things on his mind: baseball and yesterday's argument. He had a feeling that neither of his friends wanted to address those issues, so he tried to be content with Steve and Judy talking about whatever came to mind.

Judy kept trying to press Steve for details about the girl he had taken on a date. Steve was not divulging any information. Jeremy wondered if Judy was noticing how determined Steve was in avoiding her questions. His curious lack of details about these dates had to mean something. Jeremy thought again of the annoying possibility that Steve actually harbored feelings for Judy and was trying to hide it by "dating" someone else. It could also explain why Steve was constantly bugging Judy and Jeremy about their relationship. Jeremy was so caught up in his head that he didn't realize they had reached the athletic administration building at the southern corner of campus.

"Are you going to go in?" Steve asked doubtfully.

"Yeah, yeah, yeah," Jeremy said slowly.

"We'll wait out here for you," Judy chimed. "Good luck."

Jeremy only nodded his head as he entered the building, feeling nervous.

He knew that someday he would think he was being ridiculous for being so nervous at trying to get a little information. Yet, at this moment, Jeremy found himself walking past the office three times before turning himself enough to actually enter the athletic office.

"Good afternoon. Can I help you?" The receptionist asked through a fake smile and fake blonde curls.

"Uh, yeah," Jeremy said with a swallow. "I wanted to know what I need to do to be able to try out for the baseball team for next year."

"Are you wanting to talk to the Coach?" the secretary asked.

"Um, I guess so," Jeremy said. I really just wanted to get some information about walk-on try outs."

"Well, the coach's office is just through that hall," she said, motioning to her right. "He's in a meeting right now, but he has a few free minutes if you are willing to take a seat."

"Thanks, I'll do that," Jeremy said, and he sat down nervously. He continued to wipe his sweaty hands off on his jeans in anticipation of the possibility of shaking hands with the man he may have to impress later in the year. It was so much easier to be a daydreamer and remain calm while he was pitching in his basement.

After a few minutes, the coach finished his meeting and came out of his office. He was taller than the person who accompanied him. His plume of hair was silver touched with gray. His brow was high and wrinkled with age. His nose was broad and held his glasses with ease.

"Coach Thompson," the secretary said. "This young man would like to talk to you about trying out for the team next season."

Coach Thompson turned to Jeremy and extended his hand, "Is that so? What's your name son?"

"It's Jeremy, sir," Jeremy said, accepting the handshake. The coach had strong and coarse hands. The tips of his fingers were dry and appeared that they could split open at any moment.

"I assume you played in high school?" the coach asked.

"Not officially sir," Jeremy answered. "But, I know I can make it if I can just try out," he said, trying to sound more confident than he felt at the moment.

"Really," the coach said unconvinced. "I've got a few minutes.

Why don't you come in and we will talk about this for a minute."

As Jeremy walked into the office and the coach began shutting the door, he began. "There are generally two ways you get onto the team," he said, motioning Jeremy to a seat across from the desk. "First, we recruit our players while they are still in high school or occasionally from another school," the coach said, leaning back in his chair. "Second, we have walk-ons. Both require prior experience, more than just pick-up games, which I gather you don't have."

"No sir," Jeremy said softly.

"Now, obviously, I can't just say to forget about it. I have to allow you to try, even though I would strongly discourage doing so," the coach said sitting straighter in his chair.

"I understand that I need some experience in an organized setting to show that I can handle the pressure," Jeremy explained. "I've played a number of team sports in high school, to understand that situation. Game pressure I can handle." The coach nodded. "I also understand that I would not even be considered unless I have something to offer, so that I would stand out in a good way."

"That's one way of looking at it," the coach admitted.

"I also know that some positions will be harder than others for tryouts," Jeremy reasoned.

"Obviously," Coach Thompson said, encouraging Jeremy to get to the point.

"Can I ask how many pitchers you have?" Jeremy asked.

"We're losing one at the end of this season," the coach said.

"Great, you lose one and gain two," Jeremy said with a nervous smile.

"I don't quite follow you," the coach said. "Do you know someone else who wants to try out as well?"

"Well, as I understand the game, there is some strategy with using left or right handed pitches against certain batters," Jeremy explained.

"Again, that's a rather simple way of putting it," Coach Thompson said.

"At the college level of the game, you probably worry about your pitchers getting tired," Jeremy said.

"Yes, yes. I still don't understand what this has to do with gaining two pitchers," the coach said.

"I can offer something special to the game. I can pitch with either hand," Jeremy said with a new found, albeit unfamiliar, confidence. "I can switch hands according to batter. When one arm starts to get tired, I just have to warm up the other arm and start pitching again," he paused to hold onto his glimmer of confidence.

The coach remained quiet for a few moments before he burst out laughing. "You can't be serious," he said.

"Oh, I'm quite serious," Jeremy said. "I used to do it when I wrestled in high school. It completely messes up the opponent when you are doing everything right handed and then suddenly switch to be left handed and they aren't used to it," Jeremy said. "Like you said, I don't have the experience you want, but I do have something unique to bring to the team."

Still chuckling, the coach asked, "And how fast can you pitch?"

"About 82 on my right last time I was clocked," which was a slight exaggeration on the method of measuring. "But, I don't know yet about my left. I'm also here to get some advice for training."

"You really are serious," the coach said with a cough to stop laughing. "This is good. I haven't had a good laugh in a while, but I'm sorry son. It just can't be done."

"With all due respect sir, have you seen anyone try?" Jeremy asked.

"Well, no, but I'll tell you what, you think you can do it, and I'll let you come to the first day of tryouts just for the amusement."

"I guess I can't ask for anything else," Jeremy said standing. "All I need is for you to watch me pitch. My arms will do the rest of the convincing. I promise you," Jeremy said with a fierce determination.

"You are something else," the coach said, wiping his eyes. "Talk to my assistant for the information about when and where the try outs will be held."

"Thank you, sir. I will see you soon then," Jeremy said as he let himself out of the office.

"Not soon enough," he heard the coach chuckle behind him.

"Well?" Judy asked the minute that she saw Jeremy exit the building.

"I was only trying to get some simple information about tryouts," Jeremy said holding up his hands as though defending himself.

"Still, what did they say?" Judy asked.

"His secretary was the one to give me the info about tryouts," Jeremy said.

"Then what took so long?" Steve asked.

"They had me talk to the coach first," Jeremy said.

"And?" Judy said excited and fearful.

Scratching the back of his neck and fighting the urge to look down, Jeremy said, "He laughed at me."

"Told you," Steve said.

"Are you serious?" Judy asked. Her voice laced with concern.

"Yeah, I am," Jeremy said. "He thought I was kidding. The idea of walking on with no experience wasn't what did it," Jeremy admitted.

"You told them about your idea of pitching with both hands," Steve said as a statement rather than a question.

"Sorta," Jeremy replied sheepishly.

"What do you mean?" Judy asked.

"Well, I made it sound like I could pitch left and right instead of having the idea to learn," Jeremy said.

"Hmm, did he say anything else?" Judy asked.

"Yeah, he said that if I was really serious, I could show up to tryouts, because he will need a good laugh," Jeremy mumbled.

"Good, you get another guaranteed laugh later," Steve said sarcastically. "I never knew this was just to show us your real career path of becoming a comedian."

Judy slapped Steve's arm while Jeremy said, "Yeah, well, I suspect I will be getting a lot of laughs before the end." Judy looked at Steve as though daring him to make another comment. Jeremy continued, "But, in the meantime, I've got to figure out the technique of throwing left handed, because it feels really weird. Plus, I need to use the information I got from the secretary to formulate a workout routine."

"Have fun with that," Steve said, standing and hoisting his bag over his shoulder.

"I guess Steve is hungry," Judy said.

"Yeah, I am," Steve said. "But, I don't think I want to be made fun of for sitting with you two."

Jeremy warily watched Steve. Judy started to bristle, "If you are referring to either of the two things in my mind right now you'd better stop."

"I'm no mind reader, so I couldn't tell ya," Steve said as he started to walk back up the hill.

"Wait," Jeremy said as he grabbed Judy's bag and lead her after Steve. "What are you talking about?"

"I was hoping they would help you see reason; you clearly won't listen to your friends," Steve said firmly.

"That's a split vote at the moment," Jeremy said trying to keep a civil tone to the conversation.

"Stop being an idiot," Steve huffed.

Judy stopped short, because Steve's tone held no hint of playful banter. Jeremy softly spoke, "Finally? Are we seeing some honesty?"

"I'm not sorry for what I'm going to say," Steve said turning on his friends. "You are just going to ruin the smallest chance you even have. You'll squander the opportunity to be taken seriously. In the end, it won't amount to anything and you will just end up bitter and angry for not making the team."

"Steve!" Judy gasped.

"It's okay Judy." Jeremy said standing in front of her. "Don't worry about it."

"Yeah, Judy." Steve mocked. "Don't worry about it. You're not going to be the one screwing up a long shot at best."

"Where is this coming from Steve?" Jeremy asked perplexed. "Why are you getting so angry?"

Steve wouldn't offer a reason. Instead, he spun on his heal and stormed off. When Jeremy went to follow, wet fingers pulled at his forearm to stop him. Judy was crying silently, but Jeremy wasn't sure for what reason.

-ELEVEN-

How did his life suddenly become such a mess? Maybe mess was a bit of an extreme term. Jeremy certainly knew he had taken advantage of how easy his friendship with Steve and Judy had been over the last few months. They hadn't known each other before they came to college. Jeremy could hardly remember how they were introduced to each other, because it seemed insignificant. They had become such quick friends that it was as though the three of them had grown up together instead of meeting for the first time. Had Steve been trying to get to know Judy and I walked in and messed up everything? Jeremy wondered.

"So, are you still hungry?" Jeremy asked Judy in an attempt to stop thinking about possible triangles and other irrational behaviors.

"What?" Judy asked. "Are you serious?"

"Yeah, it's lunch time," Jeremy said. "Let's go if you're hungry."

"We can go eat at my place," Judy suggested.

"Let's save that for dinner and just catch something on campus for lunch," Jeremy decided for them.

The rest of the day passed like the day before. Jeremy and Judy hardly spoke to each other as they went about lunch and their various classes. They didn't share any classes today, but, by unspoken agreement, met up after each class and were not surprised that they didn't see Steve.

"Steve must be going to different sections of the class," Jeremy mused.

"Yeah, I guessed as much by his absence in the few he has with me," Judy said. "Either that or he just wants to skip classes today."

"Ridiculous thing to do," Jeremy grumbled. "More irrational behavior."

"Careful Jeremy," Judy smiled. "You're starting to sound like a psychology major."

"No chance in that Judy," Jeremy said. "I've just spent too much time with you."

"Too much time?" Judy asked.

"No," Jeremy tried to recover. "You're just rubbing off on me."

"Doesn't sound like a bad thing to happen," and they both nervously smiled.

By dinner time, Jeremy was mentally exhausted from analyzing everything about his relationship with Judy and Steve and the emotional turmoil that resulted. He had offered to help Judy with making dinner, but she insisted that he relax on the couch while she made him dinner.

Jeremy's mind drifted again as Judy's roommates came and went. The television remained off, and Jeremy pulled out some reading for a class, but he never opened the book. He closed his eyes, and, once again, thought of the last few days. Judy was different around him now. She was growing into more than just a friend. She fiercely supported his wish to try out for the team. She seemed to be genuinely interested in everything he did. He kept trying to remind himself that Judy had told him a few nights ago that she had no interest in dating him. She must be simply overcompensating to make up for the lack of Steve's support and friendship.

"Jeremy?" Judy called out an hour later. "Jeremy?" She walked over to the couch to see Jeremy completely asleep with a book on his chest unopened. "So much for homework," she whispered, brushing his hair over his forehead. She was overcome with emotion for him over the last few days. She had always considered him a close friend, but Steve's reactions were driving her closer to Jeremy. She stayed up late last night with her roommate talking about everything that had happened and seeking advice. Judy tried to rationalize that she was drawn to Jeremy, because he would need a close friend now that Steve showed his true colors.

"I think Steve is jealous of all the attention you give Jeremy," her roommate, Sharon, had said the night before. "He may be trying to hide his feelings for you."

"That's what I thought; though I never wanted to admit that to Jeremy. In fact, I denied that that was the case just a while ago," Judy agreed. "He's always teasing Jeremy that Jeremy and I are dating. I always thought Steve was testing the waters, as if we were considering it."

"Are you considering it?" Sharon asked.

"Considering which one?" Judy tried to avoid.

"There's nothing wrong with admitting it," Sharon advised.

"But, I don't want anything to change," Judy moaned.

"Anything?" Sharon asked. "Or you just don't want the relationship to get awkward?"

"I'd love for Jeremy and me to be together," Judy vocalized for the first time. She let it hang in the air while she changed for bed.

"But?" Sharon prompted.

"But, I don't know how he feels," Judy said slumping. "I just know that no matter what, he's too loyal to both Steve and me as friends. He'd never do anything to jeopardize his friendship with us."

"Meaning he'd hate if you started dating and Steve took it personally, and avoided you two, so he wouldn't be a third wheel?" Sharon raised an eyebrow. "Isn't he technically a third wheel already?"

"No!" Judy insisted.

"Judy," Sharon scolded. "He is. I've seen the three of you on campus and even in this apartment. You and Jeremy do a good job of keeping Steve involved, but there's a different way that you treat Jeremy."

"What do you mean?"

"You're clearly in love with Jeremy," Sharon smiled.

"I am not," Judy blushed, "I like him, but I can't say I love him." Sharon kept smiling as she turned down her bed.

"Love takes time, but it always starts with a deep friendship," Sharon said sounding more like a mother than a roommate.

Judy watched Jeremy sleep as she played with his hair. She smiled that he even scowled in his sleep. The increasing warmth of spring meant they had spent more time outside. Jeremy scowled so deeply that the vertical creases in his forehead were being tanned into place. Judy let a finger lightly trace the three faint lines causing the scowl to relax slightly. They exposed the white lines where the sun could not reach within the creases of a scowl.

"I can't decide," Judy heard Sharon say from the hall. "Is that the smile for a love or the smile of simply a good friend?"

Judy couldn't decide and chose not to respond.

"I think a little bit of both," Sharon frowned. "Just be careful Judy."

"I thought he was cute when we first met, but I decided it was safer to stay friends," Judy whispered without thinking. "I've never felt safer than when I am with him." Jeremy finally stirred when the timer on the oven went off, and Judy went to set the table. She had made extra for Sharon to eat with them. The two girls sat at the table while Jeremy tried to wake up and slowly walked over to the table.

"I can't believe I fell asleep," Jeremy yawned. "That was rude of me."

"You must have felt comfortable and safe," Sharon said with a knowing smile to Judy.

Jeremy caught the look, but he wasn't sure what they were referring to, as he sat at the table. "This smells good Judy," he said to redirect the conversation.

"Thank you," Judy beamed. "We call it Chilly Mac."

It doesn't look cold," Jeremy said, watching the steam distort the two faces beyond.

"It's a pun. It's just homemade chili and homemade mac and cheese mixed together," Judy explained.

"Cute," Sharon said as she dished up the three plates.

"It's a family favorite," Judy said. "Especially among my brothers."

"Easy, quick, and it has chili," Jeremy observed. "I think I see why they like it."

"They are chili fiends," Judy smiled. "This meal always gives them heartburn, but they say it is worth it if the chili is good, which it usually is."

"Sounds like my kind of crowd," Jeremy commented while taking a bite.

"Yeah, you'd probably get along with them," Judy said softly.

"You should have him meet the family," Sharon offered with a smile and was rewarded by an under table kick from Judy.

Jeremy noticed the exchanged and grunted into his food. He just wanted everything to get back to normal and not have so many awkward moments, but the fact of the matter was that his life was changing. Could he make the most of it?

Jeremy resorted to his usual standby when in an uncomfortable situation and tried to change the subject to something that would be easy for him to not get too involved in. So, he asked Sharon the typical questions college students ask; where are you from, what your major is, and other things that hopefully would allow the questioner to just listen and not have to contribute.

As Sharon talked, Jeremy and Judy's eyes met and quickly darted away from each other numerous times. He'd be foolish to deny that Judy was very attractive. Whether her attention to him was increasing or he had just failed to notice her attention to him before was not something Jeremy could judge. Having been around Sharon on a number of occasions, Jeremy was fairly certain that the looks passed between Sharon and Judy were something he had not seen before. Whatever it meant, the looks were clearly making Judy uneasy, and she blushed slightly.

Jeremy mentally slapped himself. Would it really be so bad if he and Judy became closer to each other now that Steve was apparently no longer interested in their friendship? Could Judy really be feeling more comfortable with showing her feelings for Jeremy now that Steve was out of the way? Jeremy shook himself. Who was he? He never spent this much time brooding over a relationship with a girl. Sure, he had tried to give Steve and Judy equal attention and not show any favoritism, but he had never spent so much time and energy thinking about a girl in this way. He had never slunk around glumly trying to decide what to do next and trying to interpret Judy.

Jeremy fought every day with himself about his growing feelings for Judy. She was extremely attractive. He had always seen her as attractive. He had never seriously dated anyone in his life. He had backed off when they first met, out of fear of making a good thing go to waste. He had never let a girl affect him in such a way. He dated in high school. He enjoyed having friends. He felt like something was wrong with him to spend so much time thinking about relationships as some substantial part of his life.

Jeremy was surprised at how he thought about her. His thoughts were now exciting and completely different from anything he had experienced over a girl. He wasn't filled with the pubescent cravings every high school boy feels at the sight of a pretty girl. Jeremy actually ached in his chest when she was not around. He silently hated that he felt like he had stepped out of some teen, heartsick, novel, but he did not know how else to think about Judy. He missed her the instant she was gone. He longed to hear what she would say when they met up again.

Jeremy tried to pass off his emotions as nothing but growing attraction. He was just used to being around her for long periods of the day. After the months of spending time with each other, it was entirely normal for him to begin to feel this way. He had to accept that and put an end to his inner turmoil.

"Are you okay?" Sharon asked Jeremy which pulled him out of his head.

"Yeah, the food's great," Jeremy said. "It's just filling me up quickly so I'm letting it settle."

"Judy told me about what happened with your friend," Sharon said. "I'm glad I didn't think he was cute, so you don't have to be worried about any more awkwardness than what you already bring to the table," she said with a smile as she stood to clean her plate.

"I can always tell when you're not being fully honest," Judy said to Jeremy. "What's on your mind?"

"I'm betting one of two things Judy," Sharon said with another dagger look from Judy.

"Are you going to try out for the team?" Judy asked turning back to Jeremy and trying to relax her face.

"I'm not sure. It's a fun thought, but I don't know if I will," Jeremy said finishing the last bite on his plate.

"It's because of Steve isn't it," Judy accused.

"No," Jeremy said. When Judy and Sharon glared at him, he continued, "I'm serious. I just wanted some information about try outs. I'm still undecided."

"You seemed pretty sure before," Judy reminded.

"Everything is changing," Jeremy whispered.

"Welcome to life Jeremy," Judy said. "Quit lying to yourself!" she said more forcefully. "You want to try out!"

"Why does this matter so much to you all of a sudden?" Jeremy asked with his own temper rising.

"I can't believe you'd have to ask me that," Judy huffed.

Jeremy glanced between Judy sitting at the table and Sharon standing at the sink. Sharon's expression was as though she was trying to tell Jeremy something without moving her mouth. "Are you going to answer the question?" he asked Judy.

"Because I'm your friend," Judy said quickly at Sharon's intake of breath, fearing her roommate would answer for her. "Why else would I be encouraging you?"

Sharon dropped a plate a little too loudly into the sink. "So, Steve is not a friend?" Jeremy asked.

"I'm his friend too," Judy replied hotly and stood from the table. "I cannot explain what he has against this. I can only say that he's not acting like a true friend in my opinion."

"Nor I, for what it's worth," Sharon said from the sink. Neither Jeremy nor Judy responded to her.

"But, from his view, he is looking out for me," Jeremy paused, "in some bizarre way."

"Which is why I still say that you need to try out," Judy sighed. "He could be 'looking out' for you in a better way, but we can't change what he is doing. All you can do is to try out so you can say that at least you gave it everything."

Feeling like it was his turn to stand from the table and assert himself, Jeremy stood and said, "I'm not going to make a decision right here and now in any case."

"Fine," Judy said, crossing her arms over her chest. "I've said my piece."

-TWELVE-

Jeremy and Judy continued with their mostly normal routines without the accompaniment of Steve. Jeremy scared himself when he realized just how comfortable he felt being around Judy exclusively. He slowly began to realize his weak resolve to distance himself from Judy and keep his feelings platonic when they developed the habit of attending each other's classes when the class was held in a large lecture hall. The student would pay attention while the friend would study for another class; or in Jeremy's case, panning through old books from the library on coaching baseball. Sadly, the library was Jeremy's only resource for learning the rules and techniques he would need as a pitcher. He had found a few volumes that illustrated some strength exercises for his shoulders and back for general baseball skills.

Jeremy began watching the college home games more attentively than before, particularly when there was a southpaw on the mound. He'd sneak out his cell phone and record a quick video of the pitcher. He hoped that he'd be able to slow it down on his computer to pick up some more pointers on how to pitch left handed. Judy, who normally would have chastised Jeremy for recording part of the game when such activities were prohibited, instead got into the spirit and would help shield Jeremy while he recorded.

Jeremy and Judy would occasionally see Steve on campus. His apartment was just far enough away from Judy and Jeremy that they never saw him coming from or going to campus. Whenever they saw him on campus, he was always further away and with his other "acquaintances" as Judy called them.

"We never did find out what happened on that date," Jeremy said once when he and Judy were eating rice and vegetable bowls on their way to the library. "Everything exploded before he told us," he mumbled.

"I see him from a distance with a girl every once in a while," Judy said, blowing on a fork full of food. "I'm never able to see the girl well enough to know if it is the same girl each time."

"I hope it is the same person," Jeremy said. "I hope he's found someone to be with," wanting to mean what he said though pained him that Steve was no longer a part of their life.

"Yeah, maybe now he won't be so jealous," Judy said before cutting herself off by hastily shoving the still hot food into her mouth.

"Jealous of what?" Jeremy asked as he sat on a bench outside the library.

Judy waved her hand in front of her mouth in an attempt at cooling the food scalding her tongue. "Of, you know, other couples and such," Judy said evasively.

"And such," repeated Jeremy as he scooped up the rest of his bowl.

Each night, after safely seeing Judy into her apartment, Jeremy would set up the mattress and pitch. He had scanned in every video and image of southpaw pitchers that we could find. Occasionally, he would add some content on right handed pitchers; he knew both arms would need the help. One of his roommates had let him borrow a digital video camera so Jeremy could record some of his throws. The same roommate was a film major and had the software to slow down the film, to print out Jeremy's pitch frame by frame. Jeremy desperately wished he would not always have to coach himself through to the tryouts. He didn't even know where to begin to look for an authority in pitching to give him the attention he would need.

Jeremy swam every other day and did strength exercises on the others. Judy would try to encourage him, but she didn't like sweaty gyms or the chlorine rich pools. The weight rooms on campus were constantly overrun by former high school stars trying to relive their glory days of hogging machines and admiring themselves. A few years previous the female student body united and petitioned for a private weight room; allowing them the choice over the two environments.

The days continued to warm and lengthen, though the nights still reminded everyone that winter was not far gone. As the warmth increased, so did the presence of student bodies. The grass on campus retained its dampness in some areas while others seemed to be in constant sun throughout the day. The grass grew lounging students stretching their winter forms to soak the sun into their long pants and sweaters, which they wore to protect against the stubborn cool breeze.

Jeremy and Judy felt guilty when they joined the ranks of students spreading throughout the grass of campus because they usually made fun of the awkward, computer bleached science nerds as they fumbled Frisbees across the lawn while trying to catch their falling pocket computers. The couples that were being a little too comfortable with each other as they basked in the sun as though it was a private beach were also not exempt from Judy's muttered diatribes. Steve and Jeremy used to mock the few guys who seemed to never take off their shorts no matter the temperature and showed their white legs, or the girls who'd sneak the pant legs, shirts, and sleeves up a few inches to expose tender skin to the rays of the sun. Yet, as the warmth of spring spread, Jeremy and Judy conveniently remained silent about their fellow fair-weather followers.

Jeremy and Judy refused lounging on the grass, because they saw that most of the students who did had wet spots somewhere on their clothes. Jeremy would try to snag the few wooden benches on campus that could pass for comfortable. Jeremy wanted benches that were half in the sun and half out. Judy wanted benches that were completely in the sun, and she teased Jeremy that the chemicals of the lap pool were damaging and bleaching his skin.

As Jeremy learned from the books and videos he found on pitching, he had to find a new "catcher" and retire the mattress against the wall in his apartment. He was starting to create a general deformity in the center of the mattress and could not imagine the landlord being too happy about how it was created. Jeremy still did not have anyone to rely on who would be willing to let him pitch as hard as he could. Steve had never enjoyed catching for Jeremy, so he couldn't imagine anyone else being enthusiastic in assisting him.

Jeremy started visiting the city park just next to campus during the times of the day that he didn't expect anyone else to be using it. Usually, he had to go either very early in the morning or near dusk. Occasionally, a Parks & Rec. official would come around and kick him out of the park if he was still pitching after dark. Saturdays were an extremely difficult day to find time to pitch at the few diamonds of the park. Teams and leagues of all ages ran through most of the day. If Jeremy took slightly too long with getting ready on Saturday mornings, then he ran the risk of not being able to use the diamond at all before city league practices started.

At the beginning of April, Jeremy was at the park early, trying to keep warm until the sun rose over the mountains. He jogged around the diamond and stretched his arms before gathering his glove and a bag of fresh baseballs he had bought the night before. He decided he needed a small stock of balls to throw instead of constantly walking to the backstop to retrieve the one ball he had; just another adjustment from throwing against a mattress only fifteen feet away.

Jeremy had no way to determine speed or accuracy while he was pitching against nothing but a white plate in the dirt. By the time the ball smacked against the chain link backstop, the trajectory had changed enough from the extra distance past the plate; increasing the difficulty of discerning how he was doing and where he would need improvement. Jeremy remembered, while he pitched one morning, the instruction he received while wrestling in high school. He was told to shoot through the opponent. Even though Jeremy didn't have a batter, catcher, or umpire, and was having to throw harder and further than in a normal game, he applied the wrestling wisdom to pitching. If he could develop the accuracy and speed to hit a strike zone against the backstop, it might just make it harder to hit at the plate, but, again, having never played organized baseball, he wasn't sure if the reasoning was sound.

"Kind of hard to judge your own accuracy with no one catching," a male voice said behind Jeremy as he spent his last ball in this round.

"Yeah, I know," Jeremy huffed. "It's an experiment."

"Experimenting? How so?" the voice asked as Jeremy turned.

The man was slender and tall. His hair and tanned skin betrayed his real age. Jeremy could easily tell that he was in good physical shape, which would only make him younger looking still. His temples were graying and really the only sign of age. His arms were long, yet they appeared to be proportionate to the rest of his lanky frame. His grey eyes hid beneath a strong and bushy brow.

"I've never played in an organized league," Jeremy said, feeling that it was the best place to start. "But, I play pickup with some friends and was trying to test out different styles I read about."

"I'm sure you've found that reading only teaches so much," the man said.

"Yeah, but it's hard enough to find someone to point out my mistakes, let alone teach me to throw correctly and left handed," Jeremy shrugged.

"Left?" the man asked. "I thought you were throwing right?"

"I was," Jeremy said. "I'm trying to learn how to throw with my left hand as well."

"Why left?" the man asked with sincere interest.

"My right shoulder hurts after a while, from old high school injuries," Jeremy motioned to his shoulder. "I don't want to have to stop playing after a few pitches so I want to learn how to pitch left handed."

"That's a lot of work for just pickup games," the man observed.

"Well, I'm hoping that if I can get enough time in, I can try out for the college team next season," Jeremy explained, expecting laughter like he received from Coach Thompson.

"And since you don't have any experience, you think that being able to pitch with both hands will give you the edge you need to be considered," the man said as a statement and not a question.

"That was the general idea," Jeremy nodded.

"Interesting," the man said while checking his watch. "I hope you find someone to help you out."

"Me too," Jeremy admitted, bending to pick up the empty sack to collect the spent baseballs.

"In the meantime, I've got a youth league practice here in fifteen minutes," the man said.

"Oh, sorry," Jeremy said. "I guess I do just show up when I see this is empty without regard for who has it reserved."

"You don't need to go," the man said holding up his hands. "One of the parents of the players called to say their son was sick. We're short a few at practices as it is. I could use a pitcher so I can focus on coaching."

"Are you serious?" Jeremy asked. "You want me to pitch? I'm not even sure I'm doing it right."

"You're doing well enough for what I need," the man smiled. "We don't need anything fancy or fast. Just steady for about an hour to hour and a half. Can you give me that?"

"Sure, I can try at least," Jeremy smiled excitedly.

"You'll have to be more confident than that if you want the pointers I can give you along the way," the man said, helping Jeremy collect the balls behind the plate.

"I could use any help you're willing to give me," Jeremy sighed in relief that he might get valuable instruction.

"Well, it's been a while since I pitched, but I remember the technique well enough. I do coach after all," the man offered, shrugging his right shoulder in the memory of a past life.

"Thanks, I really appreciate this Mr.?" Jeremy started.

"Richards. Adam Richards," he said holding out his hand.

Jeremy shook the hand gratefully, "Jeremy," he introduced himself.

"Let's get you properly warmed up to a catcher and see how steady you really are," Richards said. He walked over to the dugout where he had deposited his bag. He pulled out his worn, yet cared for, glove and walked deliberately to home plate.

The next fifteen minutes were some of the fastest in Jeremy's life. He wished that time would slow so he could focus on spending more time learning. Between every pitch, Mr. Richards would point out something to change for the next throw. Jeremy was starting to sweat in concentration, trying to remember everything that Richards said. He focused most when Richards pointed out that Jeremy was throwing too much with his arm and not enough with his legs.

"It's why pitchers have a windup while the rest of the team doesn't," Richards explained. "A pitcher needs to deliver at speeds faster than the rest of the team. He needs to be able to last as long as possible. His windup is where his power lies," he said walking up to the mound to demonstrate. "Drive that leg up and forward. Point the toe where you want the ball to go. Use the decline of the mound and the long step forward with that driving leg to slingshot your arm," he let lose a pitch with speed and ease. "Don't think of it as throwing if it helps. You're David against Goliath and your arm is the sling." Richards jogged back to home plate.

Jeremy sent out another pitch trying to drive his leg and slingshot his arm. The pitch was wild, but Richards roared in encouragement.

"Good," he said running after the ball.

"Good?" Jeremy snorted. "It was wild."

"Exactly," Richards said tossing the ball back. "You are too used to forcing the ball through the air. If we can get your arm used to being relaxed and like a slingshot, then we can work on the technique of manipulating the ball with your hand and arm like you should be to get the best pitch." Richards smiled. "You only know how to throw a fastball right?"

"That's correct," Jeremy admitted.

"That's fine in most cases," Richards nodded. "Many pitchers perfect a good fastball with a good strong pitch. Strong in windup and strong delivery. Their technique in their arm and hand is perfect to work harmoniously with the rest of their body." Richards crouched into position, "We'll work on the other pitches after we establish the habits you really need right now."

Jeremy nodded and shook out his shoulder once more. He noticed that some members of the team Richards coached were showing up on the bleachers after saying goodbye to their parents in the parking lot. Jeremy tried not to feel the awkwardness that was creeping in. They all appeared to be half his age and yet could most likely play the game better than he could. Jeremy shook his head in frustration and wiped away the perspiration dribbling down his brow and neck. His father had always told him that there was no place for pride in any sport. Pride consumed pure talent and squandered every situation. His father had never wanted champion athletes. "I want champion men," he'd always tell Jeremy. "I want sons that grow to be strong fathers. Men of understanding and leadership who know how to overcome their pride and learn from everyone around them."

Jeremy took one last cleansing breath and imagined the pride and self-conscious fears leave as he pitched the last pitch before the practice started.

"Better," a satisfied Richards said to Jeremy before turning towards the team. "Alright team, we're going to get started," he said looking at the team while Jeremy hung back wincing as he stretched. "But, I wanted to make a few announcements while your parents are present."

Richards started handing out printed announcements to the parents that were present and to the children whose parents had already left. "This is our schedule of games. We are normally short at practices, but Teddy is sick. You guys are a team, so you need to work with each other. So, to make sure you are ready for the season, you are here for a good practice." Richard waved Jeremy over to them. "Since we are short both pitchers, I've asked my friend here to help us out today. The good thing is that his style is not what you are used to hitting against. So, it will give you better preparation for game time. Now, ten laps, let's go," Richards blew a whistle to get the team to move.

Jeremy continued to stretch his arms while watching the team run around the diamond. "So, who's the catcher?"

"Johnson, third from the end, is our catcher. I won't have him call any pitches. Straight stuff for the majority of practice."

"That's fine," Jeremy sighed.

"There'll be a break midway. After that point, we'll be letting him practice signals. I'll review the signs we use to you. Remember, just keep it simple."

"Right, except that I still don't really know how to pitch anything other than a fastball," Jeremy reminded.

"Don't worry about it," Richards said before returning to his coaching duties. "Just a few things," he called over his shoulder. "Don't strain your hand so much when you hold the ball. That is where you are losing most of your strength in your arm. Don't strangle the ball. It needs to breathe to fly straight."

"Okay," Jeremy said. "Any more specific details on pitching other pitches?"

"Don't worry about it," Richards smiled and ran to home plate to meet his team. "You'll be fine."

"Right sure," grumbled Jeremy.

"Tired?" Richards asked at the end of practice.

"That's an understatement." Jeremy let his arms sag in fatigue. "I've never had to pitch that much for so long."

"Good. It'll hurt, but it'll be worth it in the end."

"I hope so," Jeremy winced again.

"I've got a few minutes left if you want to show me your left," Richards offered.

"That would be great," Jeremy said. "My right can use the break."

Jeremy tried his wind up for his left and threw a slow, sloppy, and wild first pitch.

"Good," Richards said before throwing the ball back.

"What?" Jeremy asked incredulously.

"I need to see what is wrong before I see what you do correct in order to help," Richards crouched into a catcher's position again.

Jeremy shook his head in disbelief and continued to throw sloppy pitches. Throw was a very generous term for what Jeremy was attempting. They barely passed as lobs in Jeremy's opinion. His one consolation was that Richards never needed to move to grab a ball.

"You are thinking too much," Richards yelled after a number of pitches. "You know how to do this already. Stop thinking about it," he said as he tossed the ball back.

Jeremy kicked at the dirt in frustration before realizing he wasn't making the corrections suggested by Richards. He took a deep breath, tried to imagine that he wasn't as tired as he felt, and sighted down his left shoulder back to home plate. He took another breath for each step of his wind up and felt his body relax.

"Better," Richards said as he caught the pitch. "You're pretty warmed up now in the left arm. Just mirror what you do when you pitch with your right hand. Drive with your leg more, relax on the ball a bit, and follow through with the sling shot."

"Not as easy as it sounds," Jeremy said shaking his arm out.

"That's why no one pitches with both hands," Richard offered with a shrug after stretching his legs.

Jeremy's next throw was harder than he had done previously with his left, and, consequently, the ball was completely uncontrolled.

"Stop thinking Jeremy. Stop focusing on how tired you are or how hard this is and just throw like you love the game above anything else."

As silly as it was to do, Jeremy closed his eyes and thought about every one of his favorite scenes from the various baseball films that adorned his DVD collection. He imagined that he was as graceful when he threw and envisioned the fluidity of the throw. While holding onto what he saw in his head, Jeremy focused on Richards and tried to ease through his next throw.

"See! You know how to do it. You just have to let your body love this game and you'll throw," Richards said smiling as he stood and walked over to Jeremy.

"But, it was controlled, because I threw slower," Jeremy said nursing his shoulders.

"First, you need to train your body how to really play baseball. Then, you can work on the speed," Richards said, dropping the ball into Jeremy's glove.

"Right," Jeremy groaned. "Assuming my arms don't give out."

"Well, it's getting late and I've got other errands to run today," Richards said, walking Jeremy over to the dugout. "Don't forget to ice those arms. They'll be sore tomorrow. More than they are right now."

"Oh, I'm well aware of the pain," Jeremy grimaced.

"How about we meet again next Saturday?" Richards asked.

"Do you need me for practice again?" Jeremy said, still unsure that he had helped with the team at all.

"No," Richards said missing Jeremy's hesitation. "You need me for practice," he said with a smile before walking way.

-THIRTEEN-

The pain in his shoulders had greatly intensified by the time Jeremy finished dinner that evening. He had tried to study during the day but could hardly hold anything in his hands. His muscles were beginning to seize in protest from being required to move any more. He felt as through his muscles from the base of his skull, across his shoulders, down his back, to his upper thighs were not his own, because they hurt in ways he did not comprehend from other sports.

While trying to find a comfortable spot with on the couch with all of his ice packs, his cell phone rang.

"Hey Judy," he mumbled into the phone.

"You sound tired," Judy said cheerily.

"I'm extremely tired," he admitted.

"Too tired to help me with something?" she pleaded.

Jeremy groaned inside, "That depends on what it is."

"I need you to proof read my story," Judy said.

"Story? I thought you were a psych major?" Jeremy asked.

"I am, but I needed some electives, so I took a creative writing class," Judy explained.

"How come I never knew about this?" Jeremy asked.

"I don't know," Judy said with a lot of background noise that could only be her gathering her stuff together to come over. "So, can you help me?"

"Only if we do it here," Jeremy said.

"Lazy. Just kidding. I figured you'd want me to come over there. See you in a bit," she said a little breathlessly.

Within moments, Jeremy was opening the door to see Judy, flushed face and beaming, standing on the other side.

Judy's eyes widened in shock, "What the heck happened to you?"

"Nice to see you too," Jeremy said, stepping aside to allow Judy to enter.

"Hi," Judy said, flustered, and pointed at his shoulders packed in ice.

"Pitching practice," Jeremy offered as the only explanation.

"Oh, good," she said a little distractedly as she spread her work across the table.

"Are you thirsty?" Jeremy asked as he shut the door.

"Yes, please," Judy offered.

Judy missed Jeremy's wincing as he tried to raise his arms to grab down some cups from the cupboard. "Water, soda, or punch?" he asked through gritted teeth.

"Just water thanks," Judy said sitting and selecting the pages she needed. "So, you had practice?"

"Yeah, I was throwing this morning at the park," Jeremy said handing the water to Judy. "When this guy shows up."

"To kick you off the mound?" Judy asked.

"That's what I thought," Jeremy said struggling to take a drink while the melting ice bag on his shoulders shifted.

"Then, what did he want?" Judy asked setting the cup down on the table away from her papers.

"He wanted to talk to me and offered me pointers in exchange for pitching for his youth league team practice."

"And you did it," she said eying the ice. "I mean, how did you do?"

"Not too bad," Jeremy shrugged. "I don't think at least. It was just a youth league practice, so I wasn't supposed to throw anything fancy."

"Did he give you any useful pointers?" Judy asked.

"Actually, yes he did. He can meet with me every Saturday to work some more," Jeremy said.

Judy asked, "Is he good at coaching?"

"He's been coaching for a number of years; he played in high school and college, and everything he taught me today really helped. I finally have someone to help me pitch in general, as well as help me learn how to pitch left handed," Jeremy said excitedly.

"Well, that is good at least," Judy said with a smile. "Every little bit helps right?"

"Yes," Jeremy said emphatically. "And right now that's all I have going for me, so I'll take it while I can."

"Do you really think that he will be able to continue to help?" Judy asked.

"I hope so," Jeremy said softly.

"Well, I hope you continue to see the help from everywhere you receive it," Judy looked down at her papers. "Here's the story for my class. Have fun and be nice. But not too nice."

"But of course," Jeremy said, holding his nose in the air and a mock accent of sophistication. Without Judy noticing, Jeremy snuck a blank sheet of paper over the top of her assignment. As she moved to sit at the couch and read, Jeremy began to scribble furiously over the blank sheet of paper. He mimed heavily crossing out lines or drawing circles around other sections and moving them around. Out of the corner of his eye, Jeremy watched Judy stiffen but try not to look over at Jeremy.

When the paper was nearly covered with ink, Jeremy finally slammed the pen down on the table, which caused Judy to jump in her seat.

"Honestly, Judy. You're no fun if you are just going to sit there and not react," Jeremy whined.

"I have to let you edit the story," Judy said stiffly without looking at Jeremy.

Jeremy quickly turned the scribbled piece of paper into an airplane and hurled it at her. Judy's hands shook as she opened the airplane and looked at him quizzically.

"I was trying to get you to react that I was scribbling so much on your story when in fact I was just scribbling on the blank piece of paper," Jeremy huffed. "Way to go on spoiling my joke."

In response, Judy crumpled the paper and threw it squarely between Jeremy's eyes before he could respond. Her face was furious as she settled herself in against the arm of the couch with her legs stretched out the length of the couch, as though to tell Jeremy that he wasn't welcome on the couch.

"You have an arm Judy," Jeremy said. "Why haven't you been teaching me?" he said with a smile. From over the rim of her book, he saw Judy smile and soften while he went through with actually editing her story.

By the time he had finished editing her story, Jeremy found Judy asleep on the couch. She had slithered down the couch to sprawl length ways with her slender body turned outward. She had slightly curled into a concave position, as though, given time, she would eventually result in the fetal position. Jeremy walked over to her and sat on the couch in the middle and leaned back against her stomach effectively pinning her in place.

"Ahh!" her sleepy cry croaked out. "What are you doing?"

"Well, you were asleep on my couch," Jeremy said with an impish smile.

"So!" Judy said trying to push Jeremy off. "That doesn't give you the right to kill me!"

"I could shred this if you're not interested," Jeremy said waving Judy's story. "It's the paper or the couch."

"Don't you dare," her eyes narrowed.

"Then don't complain about how I woke you up," Jeremy said snidely. Judy huffed, folded her arms across her chest as best she could, given the circumstances, and glared at him. "Well, at least you aren't complaining anymore." Her eyes narrowed more as Jeremy chuckled. "Overall, I think it's pretty good. I don't really know what the assignment is, so I have no idea if it meets the requirements."

"Does it flow?" Judy hissed. "Does it make a point?"

"Yes, for the most part," Jeremy said still not moving.

"For the most part?" Judy frosted as she squirmed for him to give her room on the couch.

Unrelenting in his position, Jeremy said, "Yeah, there were some parts that you seemed to have been falling asleep as you were writing, so I marked them as," he said while flipping the pages for an example, "ah, here's one. 'No idea what you are talking about.' But, other than that, what grammar things I found, I marked, but I most likely don't know what I'm talking about, and it's not my grade."

"Says the boy who speaks in run-on sentences," mumbled Judy. "That's it?" she asked as she held out her hand for the story.

"What do you mean," Jeremy asked.

"Were you awake when you read this?" Judy asked.

"Obviously," Jeremy said, clearly unable to follow her train of thought. "I can't write comments on it in my sleep."

"What about theme, plot, character development?" she raised her hands in frustration.

"The what now and the who's it?" Jeremy asked.

"Jeremy!" she whined.

"You wanted me to pay attention to that stuff?" though he could no longer hide the smile.

"Of course I did!" Judy said.

"Oh, well, in that case, you may want to look at what I left on the table," Jeremy said putting his hands behind his head and leaning back; squishing Judy into the couch even more.

"You jerk," she said nearly breathless. "Why'd you lead me on like that?"

"It was fun," Jeremy said closing his eyes. "So, it's your turn to get to work."

"Get off," she hissed menacingly. "I have brothers you know."

"Who aren't here," Jeremy said. "So what is your point?"

Judy stared at Jeremy for a moment. Then, with reflexes developed only by those who had been tormented by older brothers, Judy lashed out her hand to Jeremy's side and went for his ribs and kidneys. Squirming and yelping like a wounded animal, Jeremy flopped off the couch and onto the floor. Judy shot off the couch before Jeremy could recover any self-dignity.

"What the heck was that?" Jeremy said massaging his side.

"I said I had brothers," she seared. "Older brothers."

"Note to self," Jeremy said slowly standing, "Never to that again."

Judy smiled a victory smile as she sat at the table and looked at the plot diagrams Jeremy had created from her story.

"I knew you would probably ask me to do it anyway. So, I decided that if I could draw it out as a plot diagram after reading the story, then the story must have been able to flow," Jeremy offered. "I saw the notes on plot in your notebook and thought it might be helpful," he said softly.

"Thanks," Judy said quietly as well. "That's saved me a lot of work."

Jeremy waited as Judy reviewed the papers again before filing them away in her notebook and then into her bag.

"So, uh… are you doing anything?" Judy asked not looking up from her bag.

"Now?" Jeremy asked surprised. They had always just fallen to the habit of being around each other to hang out, so he wasn't sure why she was asking.

"Um… yeah?" Judy said, and Jeremy noticed how deep red her cheeks were becoming.

"Well, I uh," Jeremy eloquently said as he nervously adjusted the nearly-melted icepacks on his shoulders.

Judy must have taken the motion to mean that Jeremy wasn't available, because she said, "Right, sorry," with a nod to his arms.

"No… I…" Jeremy blundered, not sure what to say or how to react to the sudden awkwardness.

"No, it's … um. I've got to run," Judy said tucking some hair behind her ear.

"You sure?" Jeremy asked.

"Yeah, I just remembered that I've got to…" she said moving towards the door.

"Well, okay. I'll see you later?" Jeremy asked trying to follow but finding the kitchen table was in the way.

"Yes, see you tomorrow," Judy said fumbling on the door knob out of the kitchen and into a closet. "Oops," she said and she walked past Jeremy to get to the door that led out of the apartment altogether.

"Did you forget after all these months where the door was?" Jeremy teased.

Well, you got me flustered," she defended.

"About what?" Jeremy said lamely as she left without responding.

Jeremy turned to sit on the couch when he noticed that Judy had left the book she was reading before falling asleep. Dashing, he grabbed the book and ran after her noting, oddly, that he might just get her to stick around longer.

"Judy!" he called as he ran for the door. "Wait…"

"I forgot my," Judy had just burst through the door.

"You forgot," he said at the same time as they collided.

Their lips met for a brief moment. It was too brief to count as a kiss; especially since it was accidental, but they met just long enough that it was apparent that they both noticed that the other person had noticed what happened.

"Oh," Judy squeaked as she put her hand to her mouth.

"I'm sorry," Jeremy blundered turning red. "Did I hit your mouth?"

"Mmm," Judy mumbled behind her hand and shaking her head.

"Um, your book?" Jeremy said holding it up for her to see.

"Right," Judy said taking her hand from her mouth and trying not to look into his eyes.

"Uh, good night Judy," Jeremy said, struggling with if he should say anything more or let the moment pass.

"Right," Judy whispered. "See you later," and Jeremy wondered if a smile was fighting at the corner of her mouth.

"Do you want me to walk you back?" Jeremy offered a little too enthusiastically, seeing Judy in a new light after the accidental, almost kiss.

"No, I'm fine. Thanks anyway," she said as she turned away.

"Okay," Jeremy said softly wanting to keep her talking to him.

Judy walked away silently in the night, smiling a large smile. Jeremy stood watching her walk away, wishing again that he could understand what had caused the shift in his feelings for her and if she reciprocated.

-FOURTEEN-

The following week was filled with pregnant silences and clipped conversations between Jeremy and Judy. He disliked that his relationship was becoming more awkward than the comfort they had once enjoyed. Jeremy knew that the tension was compounded by the almost kiss, even though he had to admit that the tension had been present long before that night.

A week after the kissing incident, Jeremy was, once again, at the park to meet Richards for his second session. While Jeremy stretched and tried to remember what Richards had shown him the previous week, him walked up to Jeremy with something clearly on his mind.

"Can I ask you something?" Richards asked Jeremy while they both stretched.

"Sure," Jeremy replied.

"Why do you want to pitch?" Richards asked.

"Well," Jeremy thought, unable to formulate his words.

"Never really thought about it much have you," Richards nodded.

"It's more that I've never really had to explain it yet," Jeremy admitted. "I've only really been asked why I am insisting on pitch with both hands."

"Try," Richards suggested.

"Try?" Jeremy asked. When Richards didn't say anything, Jeremy knew he should try to verbalize everything that had gone through his head. "I regret not playing when I was younger," which was the most he had admitted to Steve or Judy.

"Did you have the chance to play?" Richards probed.

"Yeah, but I just never got into it," Jeremy said.

"Why not?" though Richards didn't need to ask, because Jeremy was about to explain.

"I was only playing because my brothers were doing it and my parents wanted me to play in little league."

"Are you doing it now to prove to them that you can do it?" Richards asked.

"No… well, maybe that's a part of it, but it's more that now I want to play."

"So what changed?"

Jeremy sighed, "I've always liked the game, but I never really showed it when I was younger, because I was hiding." Richards waited for Jeremy. "It's stupid."

"I'd like to hear it," Richards said as he led Jeremy over to the benches.

"The truth is that I was afraid of the ball," Jeremy sighed. "There was something about that white ball hurtling towards my face that scared me to death. I could never catch or hit. The one year of little league that I played in, the coach always stuck me in the middle of nowhere. I was afraid of playing, even though I liked the game and wanted to be brave. I feared that if I showed too much interest that my dad would force me to play more often when I was just terrified of catching the ball." Jeremy sat in silence knowing that Richards wasn't going to jump in very often.

"The one time that I actually hit the ball it was an accident. I almost never got walked, and I nearly always struck out," Jeremy said, digging his toe into the dirt. "I just couldn't get the hang of playing. I made a ton of excuses that the bat was too heavy, the helmet too big, so I couldn't see. Anything just to explain why I couldn't play. My parents tried one more year, but I got the chicken pox and missed the whole season after the first week of practice."

"Sounds like redemption to me," Richards said.

"I already admitted that is part of why I'm doing this," Jeremy huffed. "But, I figured it was ridiculous that I loved to watch the game but would never join in when my friends played. I knew I could pitch fairly well for having never played, but I couldn't catch the ball when they threw it back."

"You knew you could throw?" Richards was curious.

"My eldest brother taught me how to pitch in hopes that my confidence would increase. It did help a little, but it didn't last.

"I'm not doing this for that reason only. I was forced into playing once in PE in high school, and everyone had to try at being pitcher and batter, so I did and forgot that we were doing slow pitch softball," he swallowed sheepishly. "Well, I pitched regular and the catcher was the PE teacher and the coach of the softball team. He said it stung, but he could have been trying to be encouraging. It felt good," Jeremy said, remembering. "I confided in a friend of mine that I sucked at baseball, had never really learned how to play and asked if he'd help me out. He agreed, and I started getting into pickup games by the time I came to college. Pretty soon, I got better and was pitching most of the time, as long as my shoulder wouldn't give out."

"Is that how you got the idea for trying out for the team?" Richards asked.

"Not exactly. I haven't pitched for the intramural team I was on," Jeremy explained. "It's really a recent idea about trying out for the team. We had an intramural game recently, and I pitched very briefly.

As a joke, my friend suggested I try out for the team," Jeremy paused. "Except now he thinks I'm a fool for trying out, because I apparently don't have a chance at pitching with both hands and surviving the training."

"So, we are back to you proving your worth," Richards summarized. "You are proving to your parents and siblings that they didn't waste their time on you when you were young. You are proving to yourself that you can do this, and you are trying to prove your friend wrong by hoping to be able to make the team."

"I just want to be able to get through tryouts," Jeremy sighed. "I just want to be able to say that I tried."

"Well, technically, this is trying." Richards pointed out. "Why not call it quits now and say that you tried."

"Because it wouldn't be the same for me," Jeremy said. "It doesn't end for me until I get to the tryouts. They are going to have to physically restrain me from getting to those tryouts."

"That's better," Richards said with a trace of a smile.

"What's better?" Jeremy asked.

"I wanted to know a bit more about you before we started your training," Richards said, standing to walk to the mound. "While we need to teach you some technique, I have to point out some things about your windup. It's too loose and long. It gives any runners too much time to steal a base. You need to be quicker."

"Quick can hurt," Jeremy said.

"It hurts, because you have been doing it wrong this whole time," Richards smiled. "If you do it the right way, you will have an added strength to your pitch. We'll help convert the slingshot movement to be the end of the coiled spring."

"And it won't hurt anymore?" Jeremy asked disbelieving.

"Oh, it'll hurt until you get used to the correct way of pitching, and then it'll hurt from exertion," Richards corrected.

"No pain no gain right?" Jeremy said.

"Exactly. Now, watch me," Richards said. He stretched his right arm for a few minutes and then demonstrated a tight strike. "I'll do it again, slower and a few more times. Watch carefully, so that you can see what I am doing. Focus only on the windup, not the actual pitch," Richards instructed before pitching a few more times.

Jeremy tried to ignore everything else and just focus on each element of the windup in turn. For one pitch, all he looked at were the feet. During another pitch Jeremy focused on posture. The third pitch, Jeremy watched how he kicked up his leg before planting it to the ground. Every pitch brought new insight to Jeremy.

"Ready for your turn?" Richards asked.

Still trying to focus on what he had seen, Jeremy nodded and then exchanged places. Focusing on the memories of the movements, Jeremy closed his eyes and envisioned his body moving the same way before he allowed his body to actually move. Slowing the process once more in his head, he walked through the motions and then carried them out.

"Not bad, but still too loose," Richards said. "The power comes more from your legs. You don't need to flail around so much with your arms."

Nodding his comprehension, Jeremy tried again. This time, however, he over compensated and nearly cried out in pain as he let the ball fly.

"You obviously tensed up a bit too much on that one," Richards smiled, as though at Jeremy's pain. "You still need the arm to sling over the ball; remember, the power is not coming from your arm and shoulder. That's why your arm hurts so badly when you throw," Richards said demonstrating in slow motion, "You only throw with your arm and shoulder. You haven't been giving enough from your legs. Last week you did, but you have forgotten after years of throwing incorrectly."

"I don't really understand how to change the balance of power for the throw to be in my legs," Jeremy said. "It feels right that I should be throwing with everything in my arm."

"It's not so much of a change of balance as much as sharing the responsibility and action. You will obviously still need to throw hard with your arm, but it won't tire so quickly and painfully, because you will be adding extra support to the throw by involving the rest of your body, and especially your leg. By having the rest of your body become part of the pitch, you will throw harder, faster, and more accurately."

As though to prove his point, Richards demonstrated a full speed pitch after only throwing with his arm. The difference was clear to Jeremy. It was just a matter of forcing his body to learn a new way of doing something. There was no argument that this new way was the correct way.

As Jeremy pitched, trying to incorporate everything that Richards had shown him, Richards called out more tips. Richards had set up a net to catch the balls, so he could stand next to Jeremy and get a better angle on what Jeremy needed to correct.

"Point with the toe as you step out," Richards called. "It's more than just a step." Richards demonstrated. "Lift up high with the leg and knee and then drive it forward in a lunge."

Jeremy pitched again, beginning to feel improvement while listening to Richards yell, "Remember, you are a spring. Coil and release that energy." Jeremy started to feel comfortable with his windup and started throw more of his strength into each pitch. "Explode in a controlled manner," Richards chastised when Jeremy became too confident. "Drive the leg, swing the arm around and release," Richards chanted with each pitch.

After a few more pitches, Richards interrupted, "Watch again." Jeremy moved off the mound to allow Richards room. "Watch how where I point my toe will tell a lot about where the ball will end up."

While Richards exaggerated the movement for Jeremy's benefit,

Jeremy noted the extreme detail of Richards driving foot. The difference in this pitch was finally noticing the trailing leg and how it could affect the whole body and ultimately the pitch. "I think I see it," Jeremy said contemplatively.

"We'll see if you do," Richards said, tossing a ball to Jeremy.

Concentrating more on his legs than anything else, Jeremy breathed in on the windup and exhaled in the release of the throw. His legs propelled his arm and Jeremy instantly knew something was different with this pitch. His whole body was low and propelled by the force driven from his legs.

"WHOOOHOOO!" Richards hollered. "Now that is more like it. Next time keep your eyes open longer through the pitch, and you will be able to aim better," he said with a smile, running to the catcher's position. "Let's do that again."

"It was better?" Jeremy asked. Though he had felt it was an improvement, he needed confirmation.

"Keep your eyes open and find out." Richards crouched after removing the catching net. Jeremy tried to calm his breathing and remember what he had done differently and to recall that distinct new feel to the throw. He wound up again, envisioning his body as a coiled spring. Just before he started to throw with his arm, Jeremy drove high and forward with this left leg. His arm sliced through the air, propelling the ball from his hand as his right foot became free from the ground. Jeremy could not believe that the resultant pitch he witnessed had been thrown by him.

"See? Now the fun begins," Richards said with a smile at Jeremy's surprised expression. "You've got a full bag of balls there so let's get to work."

Richards had Jeremy pitch straight and simple for the remainder of the hour. Jeremy noticed how easily the movements were being integrated into this method. Occasionally, he would focus too much, or not enough, and the ball would fly wild. Richards hardly needed to correct Jeremy in these moments, and he could see that Jeremy was slowly beginning to understand what he had done wrong. Jeremy could feel the pull and fatigue in his right arm halfway through their workout, yet the pain wasn't the same as before. He now understood what Richards meant about learning the correct method for pitching.

Jeremy's hand and arm were tingling by the time they called an end to their practice. As they packed up their equipment to walk back to their cars, Jeremy asked, "So, when do we begin on the left hand?"

"Not, yet. We still need to get this improved style to be second nature with you before teaching you how to then convert it into your left hand," Richards said, deflating Jeremy. "But, based on how quickly you learned today, and if you keep working as well as you are, we should be able to start soon on the left."

"Thank you for your help," Jeremy said. "I don't think I would have ever made this level of progress on my own."

"Maybe you would have," Richards commented. "But, probably not as quickly."

"Well, thanks again," Jeremy said.

"Not a problem. As long as you keep showing up with a desire to improve, I will always help. Speaking of which," Richards said, pulling a folder from the passenger seat of his car. "Here's a workout and diet routine for when you are not pitching. It is designed to help strengthen your arm, keeping it loose, and preventing injury," he said handing the folder to Jeremy. "I've adjusted everything you do in here to incorporate your left arm as well. While we work on your right arm style, we need to prepare your left until the time comes to start pitching with the left."

Jeremy didn't say anything as he stared at the folder with mixed emotions.

"Is something wrong?" Richards asked.

"Why are you so willing to help me out with this? You hardly know me," Jeremy asked.

"Don't you want the help?" Richards smiled; the crow's feet of his eyes appearing.

"Of course," Jeremy said hurriedly. "It's better than I could have hoped for this journey. I'm just curious."

"We're not that different, you and I," Richards said softly. "See you next week," and he climbed into his car to leave Jeremy deep in thought.

-FIFTEEN-

A few weeks later, Jeremy and Judy were frantically attempting to pass their final exams for the semester. Judy had no hesitation in admitting that she was markedly more frantic about her finals than Jeremy. Campus litter slightly increased during the last week of the semester, because students were prone to shuffle through stacks of notes, occasionally losing a scrap, which tumbled across the pavement and became embedded in the bushes.

"I just know that I will never be able to remember the order he gave in class," Judy huffed, fumbling with her papers, as Jeremy directed them through campus.

"I'm sure you will do fine," Jeremy said, so distracted during finals week from studying that he couldn't remember the professor to which Judy was referring.

"Thank you," she said, distracted in her notes. "Now, what are the three…"

"Judy," Jeremy groaned as the testing center came into view. "If we don't know it now we won't ever know it."

"Not true, it could be the one thing that we need that will stick out in our minds," Judy retorted.

"Right, the one thing that sticks and drives out the rest. Thanks, I'll get maybe a half a percent on this final," Jeremy grumbled.

"That would be sadly hilarious," Judy giggled. "I would tease you mercilessly."

"I have no doubts about that," Jeremy smiled at having successfully eased Judy's temperament; if just for a moment. Jeremy held the door to the testing center open for Judy who passed through with her nose buried into her notes once again.

The testing center was a building on campus that was used solely for administering exams for the university. Professors filed a copy of their test, so that their students could show up during an assigned block of time to take the exam. This service enabled the students to work around their schedules and to procrastinate requesting the exam before the cut-off time. During finals weeks, neighboring buildings on campus became overflow testing centers for specific courses known for having large class sizes.

Jeremy tried avoiding the testing center in his selection of professors. Some professors refused to use the testing center and preferred to administer the test during the regularly scheduled class time in the classroom. Jeremy hated tests in general but would rather take the test in a classroom, if given the opportunity.

As they queued up in the line to request their exams and pulled out their student ID cards Jeremy asked, "Just think, in about an hour, we will be done for the semester."

"I know," Judy sighed exaggeratedly. "I am so ready to be done."

"And we get to really enjoy the baseball game tonight, knowing the semester is over," Jeremy reminded.

"Are you ready?" Judy asked as she looked up at the counter.

"For the game? Absolutely," Jeremy smiled.

"I meant the test," Judy said.

"Ready for it to be over," Jeremy grumbled as his stomach churned in anxiety just as the helper at the counter motioned him up to the computer. He handed her his ID card, which she mechanically swiped through the reader before handing it back.

"Biology?" the helper asked.

"Unfortunately yes," Jeremy smiled at the attendant.

The helper handed him his test packet without offering any response to his flippancy, "Your answer sheet will print at the end of the counter," she said motioning over his shoulder for the next person.

"Here goes everything," Judy said having retrieved her exam answer sheet just before Jeremy.

"Good luck," Jeremy said with sweaty hands on his pencil as they stood close together to pass through the door to the testing room.

"Yeah, you too," Judy said making a movement as though to kiss Jeremy on the cheek before recovering herself and hurrying into the testing room. He couldn't help but notice the redness growing from her cheeks to the back of her neck.

Jeremy and Judy found some seats relatively near each other. Judy's row was set perpendicular to Jeremy's, which allow him to stare at her profile. Five minutes had passed from when Jeremy sat down before he actually started his test. He had been completely caught up at gazing at Judy. Jeremy had always felt that she was attractive. However, the last few weeks were opening his eyes to her to see how extremely attractive she was.

Jeremy watched as her tongue poked slightly between her lips as she concentrated. He could tell when she caught herself doing this, because her tongue would shoot back while her hand came up to rub at her lips. Jeremy watched as her head bowed in frustration over her test and a waterfall of her hair cascaded down to block his view of her cheeks and eyes. Jeremy pulled his eyes away then and turned to his test. He didn't see the words on the papers. The text meshed together to make a black and white image of Judy's profile. Shaking himself, Jeremy, set to work on his exam.

The most distracting aspects of taking a test in the testing center for Jeremy were the varying schedules and tests going on around them. Students came and went around him in the tightly packed desks. Proctors would walk up and down the aisles to watch for cheating. Jeremy was distracted whenever anyone passed his desk. He would stop his test just long enough to glance up and catch the sight of Judy a few feet away. He would frustratingly force himself to look back at his test.

Jeremy never liked to take too long on a test. He felt that each test had a happy medium in length. If he took it took quickly or slowly, then his performance on the exam would decrease. As such, whenever Jeremy and Judy took exams at the same time, he always finished before her. Judy thought that she could never take enough time on an exam. Jeremy had been trying to remind her that their professor said that the part of their final that could only be taken in the testing center should not take more than an hour.

After 45 minutes, Jeremy quietly rose from his desk and left the testing center, after quickly double checking that he hadn't skipped a line in the answer sheet. He turned in his test and answer sheet to the counter outside the testing room and walked down the stairs to the main level.

The main level of the testing center had television displays spaced in random intervals near the ceiling. They displayed the last five digits of a student ID number and the score of their answer sheet. Because part of their final had been open-ended questions, the score displayed would only give them a glimpse at a possible final exam score. Jeremy nodded at the screen and then went outside to wait on a bench for Judy to finish her exam.

Jeremy sat in the early afternoon sun with his eyes closed and his hands behind his head. He had been dreaming and planning for this moment for a few weeks. He had planned to sit relaxed for a moment, listening to the sounds of students bustling around him in the afternoon frantically trying to finish their finals before the end of the day. Surprisingly, Jeremy didn't find it as soothing and relaxing as he had planned. He was still thinking about Judy. Somehow, the successes in his Saturday sessions with Richards, and the completion of his last final exam for the semester, disappeared in an influx of emotion for Judy.

They had always found time to be around each other while studying late into the night. Jeremy had noticed that on a friendship scale this would normally equate to something deep and personal. However, their conversations over the last week had been completely dominated in quizzing each other on review questions and not much on friendly conversation. He felt empty when she wasn't around, which was completely ridiculous, because they weren't even dating. Jeremy was completely aware of how much the thought of them not dating upset him. When had that changed?

"What's with the scowl?" Judy voice broke through his thoughts. "I expected to see you doing cartwheels now that finals are over," she said smiling softly.

"I was just sitting in my head," Jeremy mumbled as he stood. "So, how'd you do?" he asked in an attempt at recovering the mood.

"I got a B plus!" she said squealing. "I never thought I'd get that high."

"And that's without the open-ended part being graded. Which, in your case, always helps," Jeremy said. "Especially since the test is graded where if you get at least a B plus on the multiple choice, you are nearly guaranteed to get an A for the final and ultimately the course."

"That's right. Sweet!" she said as she hugged Jeremy, like she had never done before. "That is really exciting! Oh, I'm so happy I could kiss you," and her eyes widened and her hands flew to her mouth. "I can't believe I said that. That's not something I normally say. I sound like I'm out of a cheesy movie. I'm just so happy that I could do something…"

"Without realizing what you were doing?" Jeremy offered, with his hands getting hot again.

"Yeah, um, that's it," Judy said blushing horribly.

"What's the psychology term for that," Jeremy teased.

"Be quiet," she said. "What did you get on the exam?" she asked too emphatically.

"Just an average B," Jeremy said.

"Just your average B?" she mocked. "Don't be so modest. Here I was stressing out about the test, and you are all cool as cool, not worried at all and you get a B."

"I was worried," Jeremy smiled. "Just not as much as you."

"Yeah, well, it paid off didn't it?" Judy said defensively.

"Sure did," Jeremy said. "Especially because now we are done," Jeremy said with a sly smile to Judy as they walked. "How about I take you out to eat before the game?" he tried to make it sound more like a suggestion than a nervous question and betray his calm exterior.

"Are you taking me on a date?" Judy asked excitedly.

"I guess I am," Jeremy said, his knees buckling. It was ridiculous how nervous he was after so much time together. He wasn't acting like himself, "Is that okay?"

"Let me let you in on a little bit of a secret," Judy said in a tone of confidence and collection that surprised Jeremy. "I've wanted you to ask me out on a date for a long time."

"Then, I'm asking you out," Jeremy smiled nervously.

"I accept," Judy said as she slipped her arm through Jeremy's. "It'll have to be quick, because I know you want to get to the game."

"I think we can make an exception," Jeremy said leading her towards the south corner of campus.

"But, you never miss the National Anthem at the game!"

"We may still make it to the whole thing," Jeremy thought.

"Oh, so a romantic date at the vending machine," Judy concluded.

"No, I don't think so," Jeremy laughed. "I've been saving up and we're going to the little pizza joint on the corner of campus."

"Oooh, good choice," Judy said. "When I was growing up, we used to celebrate the end of school with pizza."

"Well then, shall we go?" Jeremy said completely surprised at how he was acting and how much he was enjoying this new personality that had completely taken over both him and Judy.

"This smells so good," Judy sighed as the pizza was placed before them.

"Yeah, Steve and I would reward ourselves after tests and projects by coming here to eat and then over to the museum part of the Athletic Building," Jeremy said.

"We have a museum?" Judy asked.

"At least three," Jeremy said. "Technically four or five. Well, technically, only one is listed as a museum. The rest are museum slash monument slash place of remembrance."

"Nicely worded," Judy teased through her napkin.

Then ticking the exhibits off on his greasy fingers, he said, "There's the Life Science Museum by the dorms, the Art museum by the Fine Arts building, the Sports museum, which is small and more like a Hall of Fame, and the almost museums are the Special Collections in the basement of the library and the lobby of the science center," Jeremy said.

"Oh, yeah, the dinosaur is in there," Judy said. "I never thought of that as a museum of sorts."

"Well, there are a number of exhibits to view in just that lobby, but that is why I said they were almost museums," Jeremy said taking another slice.

"So, do we have time to go to the Hall of Fame?" Judy asked, taking a drink from her soda.

"I think we may," Jeremy calculated the remains of the pizza.

"I'm so glad the semester is over," Judy said randomly.

"This is a great way to celebrate," Jeremy said.

"Mmmmm hmmmm," said Judy through a mouthful of pizza.

"We'll have to make this quick if we want to make it to the game on time," Jeremy said as they hustled with full stomachs towards the student athletic building. "Since we only have a few minutes, I thought I would show you the important stuff. We can come back another time for the rest." Jeremy practically pulled her up the flights of stairs to the second level and into a nook. "The baseball Hall of Fame for our school," he said with dignity to Judy's smiles. "My personal favorite," he said pointing to a section of the far wall. "Kendrick D. Abernathy."

"What did he do?" Judy asked though she could have read it herself.

"No one here has pitched more innings, won more games, or thrown more no hitters than Abernathy," Jeremy said in awe.

"And you want to be the next on the wall," Judy surmised.

Chuckling, Jeremy said, "Not really. I just want to make it on the team and be someone who matters."

"Well, even if you don't make it on the team, you matter," Judy said softly.

"Yeah?" Jeremy asked looking at her.

"Of course. You didn't know that?" Judy asked seriously.

"Well, I know I've got friends and family, but I'm not following you." Jeremy said in response to Judy's expression.

"I wasn't entirely honest with you earlier about wanting you to ask me on a date," Judy said. "It wasn't the whole truth."

"So, what is?" Jeremy prompted.

"Jeremy, I'm tired of being a friend," she sighed. "I'm tired of waiting for you to see that."

Not expecting this response, Jeremy said, "Okay, now I really don't follow you."

"I'm tired of only being a friend," Judy said standing closer to Jeremy.

He backed up a step, "Oh, that. Yeah, I think I noticed that."

She stepped closer again, "And?"

Stepping back again and feeling that the air was remarkably warm he said, "What brought this on?"

"We spend a lot of time together," Judy said closing the gap.

"I know, but after all this time, why bring it up now?" Jeremy asked stepping almost to the wall of the baseball nook.

"Jeremy, I just told you what brought it on," Judy said stepping closer.

"Judy, I have noticed, and you must have noticed that I," Jeremy said and swallowed.

"Yes?"

"I don't want this to be just a fling," he said and stepped back.

"Nor do I," she said stepping forward. "I've hoped for the long haul. I know that can be a lot to take in."

"Strangely enough, no, it's not," Jeremy said, his back against the wall. "But, we should just take everything one step at a time."

"We have been doing that for months," Judy sighed. "We've just been stuck at one step for too long now." She stood very close. Close enough that her breath tickled his nose as she looked up at him.

"I guess, we do spend a lot of time together," Jeremy reasoned. "And, we have been spending even less time away from each other."

"That we do," she whispered and Jeremy could feel the light traces of her fingertips along his hands. He didn't know what to do. He was panicking over his sweaty hands. She'd notice the sweat if he didn't do something, so he moved his hands to try to dry them off.

"So, I guess, it just follows reason that we should consider something more," he said trying to remain calm, though his mind kept reminding him that they were in a nook in a public building.

"While reason has nothing to do with this," Judy said, "It does have a point. So how do you suggest we resolve this?"

Jeremy had been holding his breath and let it out slowly hoping it didn't stink. She didn't recoil, "Well, I guess now is as good as a time as any to tell you that I," he swallowed and she looked expectantly up at him. "That I found you to be very attractive from the beginning, but I had just wanted to be friends."

"I didn't want to rush into anything either. I thought you were Steve's wingman," Judy admitted with a laugh. "I wanted to be friends with you first, before becoming a couple."

"Oh, right. Makes sense. Me too," Jeremy stumbled and wished the wall gave him more room.

"So, how do you feel about that?" Judy asked trying to hide her smile.

"About what? Being a couple?" Jeremy asked, vaguely aware that this could have been a very ridiculous conversation to witness. No one was as straight forward as Judy.

"Yes," Judy whispered, breathless in anticipation.

Jeremy thought for a second. A second was all it took. He saw her taking the test, saw her reading by his side in his apartment, falling asleep during a movie under a blanket while he ate popcorn, walking in the early spring morning in a skirt and the wind in her hair. He saw her eyes and finally admitted the truth to himself. He wanted to be with her. He had always wanted to be with her.

"It's all I want right now. I can't hide it any longer," Jeremy breathed.

"Good answer," she smiled. "Now that that is out of the way. There is one last thing," she said wryly.

"What's that?" Jeremy asked puzzled. He wondered if she would ever stop catching him off guard.

"This," she said and surprised him yet again.

She reached her arms around his neck. He hadn't noticed that her hands had moved up his arms; it had felt so natural. Her lips met his. Had he thought about kissing her, he would have imagined soft, tender lips lighting on his mouth like whipped cream. Her lips were hard with urgency from withholding this feeling for so long.

Breathless with surprise, he said when they parted, "I sure hope that's not the last thing," and smiled at his own openness in the situation. He definitely didn't know this side of himself, but, he liked it.

"Oh, I don't think it will be," Judy was confident as she kissed him again.

-SIXTEEN-

Jeremy was not upset in the slightest that they were late to the game that evening. It was amazing to him that a simple kiss was all that was required to change his entire outlook on life. It really began with the accidental kiss a few weeks prior. Jeremy hadn't been able to focus on much else and now, he felt like he could breathe. The wedge between them was healed now that they were finally open with how they felt.

Even though it was late spring, the evenings at the ball park could still get chilly in the bleachers. Jeremy and Judy took their usual spot along the third baseline, which put them in less shelter and more wind. They had stopped briefly at Jeremy's apartment to grab a blanket to keep away the worst of the wind. Judy snuggled her way, unashamed, into Jeremy arms. The warmth from her body penetrated more than just his skin. Neither of them seemed to pay much attention to the game. Judy fingers found Jeremy's under the blanket, and they held on firmly as though she no longer could speak and could only communicate through touch.

They enjoyed a good laugh when, during the change of innings, the camera crew panned around the stadium in search of couples to display on the scoreboard while playing "They Call it Puppy Love." The cameramen apparently thought they were the best couple because they were snuggled close together under a blanket bearing the university logo and colors. Judy rewarded the cameramen's attention by craning up to kiss Jeremy on the cheek while bubble hearts burst across the score board. Jeremy pretended to hide under the blanket.

"Well, you bought dinner, so let me buy desert," Judy said standing and tucking the blanket around Jeremy. "I'll be right back," she said kissing him on the cheek.

"You missed," Jeremy said.

Judy smiled as she bent over to kiss him on the mouth. "It's too early in our relationship to be so picky," she said walking away with a smile.

Judy walked most of the way to the concessions with a smile on her face. It had been a long year trying to hide her feelings. She had originally met Jeremy and Steve at the beginning of summer term the June before. They became friends instantly, but she had always been more interested in Jeremy than she was in Steve. She had been torn when Steve decided to let a small disagreement separate him from them. She wanted Steve to still be a friend but was glad for the extra time she had with Jeremy. The last few months, and especially the last few weeks, had been really hard for Judy. She had not been sure that she had the patience required to wait for Jeremy to come around and open up with her.

Their accidental, almost first kiss had been exciting, to say the least. Just when she had been about to give up hope that Jeremy would ever acknowledge her devotion to him, he was suddenly different. He joked and flirted with her, which was uncommon for him. Then he tried to ask her out that night. She had only refused him at first, because she was frustrated with him. Now, she could be completely content.

"Hi, two cans of soda and a bag of sunflower seeds," Judy said to the concessions stand. She gathered the products and turned to go back to the stands. On her way back, she bumped into someone who was yelling in the portal at a bad call from the umpire.

"Sorry," Steve said without paying attention to who it was that he was blocking in the portal.

"Steve?" Judy said surprised.

"Oh, hey Judy," Steve said unceremoniously. "I didn't realize that was you."

"It's okay," Judy admitted, shifting the frosted cans of soda.

"I mean, I saw you earlier up there with," Steve said pointed to the bleachers along the third baseline.

"Jeremy," Judy prompted.

"Yeah, well," Steve shifted.

"Is that why you are down here?" Judy accused. "Didn't want to sit with us? All because he wants to try out?"

"That's not all he apparently is trying out," Steve shot back.

"Steve!" Judy said with tears prickling in her eyes. She wished she hadn't bought the snacks, because then her hands would be free to slap.

"I'm sorry," Steve said obviously not. "That's not directed at you."

"Yes it is!" Judy seethed.

"No, it's not," Steve said emphatically. "I've got nothing against talking to you. It's him."

"You are such a child," Judy shook her head. "As you seem to have noticed, we're together now. So, anything you have against him is against me too."

"I didn't think you were married," Steve spat.

"We don't have to be for me to care about him," Judy said throwing her chin up. "I don't appreciate the remarks you make about him or us dating."

"Well, that's just great. Now he'll have someone to comfort him when he makes a fool of himself."

"What is your problem?" Judy shoved with the sodas. "Why have you been acting this way over such a simple idea?"

"Because it's a ridiculous idea!" yelled Steve, causing people around them to debate watching the game or their argument.

"So that justifies breaking a friendship," mocked Judy. "For the record, I've done nothing but stick up for you and try to get him to at least talk to you, but it seems I was wasting my time."

"Well, don't let me take any more of your time. Enjoy your private box with your boy," spat Steve.

"Our spot Steve. Ours. That was where you sat with us every game too. I chose it hoping you would show up and we could all be friends again," Judy said, tears flowing freely.

"Well, I don't want to be pissed off at you two while I'm trying to enjoy a game," said Steve as he started to move away.

"Too late for that," Judy sniffed.

"Judy?" Jeremy had just come around the corner to see Judy in tears and Steve fuming.

"Great," Steve said softly but obviously loud enough to be intentionally heard by Jeremy and Judy.

"Steve!" Jeremy sounded almost shocked. "Uh, how's it going? You coming up to sit with us?" he asked, obviously trying to be civil and move beyond the past weeks.

"Yep. But, I don't want to be the third wheel in the cuddle fest, so maybe I shouldn't," Steve said sarcastically. Jeremy's face was in complete surprise. "No retort?" sneered Steve. "How long man? Figure you'd just hide it from me?"

"Hide? Why would I hide anything from you?" Jeremy asked visibly flustered.

"I've only been asking for nearly the entire time we knew each other, but you seemed to be pretty busy, too busy to need a regular friend and not one with benefits," Steve said, deciding he'd rather leave the game and began walking away.

Jeremy hurried after him and away from the general public. "Not need a friend? Of course I did!" Jeremy said angrily. "That's why I opened up to you in the first place."

"Clearly leaving out some things," Steve said over his shoulder. "Just how long were you two together before thinking of telling me, you know your 'friend'?"

"It honestly happened this afternoon," Judy cried next to Jeremy's shoulder. "Thanks to you really. You helped me at least to admit from the beginning that I like Jeremy."

Steve stiffened, "Yeah?"

"Yes, Steve," Jeremy said. "I know I was bugged by it most of the time, but it was always working on me. I always thought about what would happened to the three of us if Judy and I got together."

"So you were trying to split it up all along," Steve accused.

"Wow, that was childish," Jeremy said.

"Ah, how cute, you even think alike," Steve said.

"All I'm saying is that I may not have clued into it if you hadn't brought it up," Jeremy said trying to regain some composure.

"No, you wouldn't have clued in." Steve pounded a finger into Jeremy's chest. "Because you never clued into anything that was around you. I've been trying to get you to clue in on how you are going to humiliate yourself, and you won't accept it, and now, you are going to drag Judy down to," he spat.

"I'm sorry I didn't feel the same way about you," Judy said softly. "I was blinded by Jeremy."

"Yeah well, you weren't the only one that was blind," Jeremy said. "I didn't start to make sense of any of this until your completely irrational response to me wanting to try out. It wasn't really about trying out after all was it? It was that I was doing something again that was drawing Judy's attention away from you!"

"I've only got one thing you need to know Jeremy," Steve shook before slugging Jeremy in the jaw.

"JEREMY!" Judy cried as Jeremy fell back off balance.

Humiliated beyond belief, Jeremy stood back up from the ground wanting to rub his jaw but stubbornly not wanting to give Steve the satisfaction. "I'm alright," Jeremy said.

"It's always about you!" Steve said, fist cocked for another round. "It was always about you. We always had to be interested in your ideas and dreams. And it will be only about you." Steve hissed. "Judy, he doesn't deserve you, and you deserve better than him. He'll only chase one dream after another, and leave you out to dry. First it was bouncing through majors. How many? Four? Now, it's this ridiculous idea of pitching?" Steve said staring at Judy. "He'll never wake up and focus on what really matters," he said trying to reach for her hands.

"Get away," Judy said, shocked. "I don't know you. You aren't the Steve I remember. This is completely different and uglier than anything you were before." Judy shuttered. "I don't know what has happened to you. I don't know if I'll ever understand, but you need to figure this out on your own. We're tired of waiting for you to be reasonable," she wasn't sobbing anymore, but the tears still cut down her cheeks.

Steve didn't say anything else as he stared imploringly at Judy. She stepped back to take Jeremy's hand and Steve stormed out of the ball park.

"I'm sorry you had to be part of this," Jeremy said softly holding her shoulders.

"I'm sorry, I kind of started it," Judy said.

"No, maybe he's right. Maybe I have been selfish from the beginning," Jeremy said shaken.

"No you haven't. I was being selfish by trying to get us all to be friends again when he's hurt. Maybe I should stop and leave things alone," Judy said moodily as she picked up the dropped soda cans.

"What? No way. Life is just getting good finally," Jeremy said. Judy raised an eyebrow at him. "Okay, so things between me and Steve aren't great, but I've got you. Not just my best friend but something so much more."

"At what cost?" Judy frowned. "I'm sorry I ruined the game."

"I didn't see you out on the field," Jeremy said directing her back to the portal. "The game is still there, waiting for us. Unless you are one of the players skipping the game, or you've paid off the umpires, you can't ruin the game. Let's go have some fun," he said smiling despite the rising lump of his jaw.

"Okay," Judy said holding a semi-chilled can to his jaw.

They quietly made their way back up to their seats and sat silently eating sunflower seeds, appearing to watch the game. Neither spoke or commented on the game. Had they but spoken to each other, they would have learned that they were both thinking some of the same things.

They had been correct in their guesses a month ago that Steve had been interested in Judy. Jeremy was still unable to put together how his trying out for the baseball team meant that Steve wouldn't have a chance with Judy. Had he, Jeremy, really been so entirely self-consuming that he had missed hints sent by Steve about his feelings toward Judy?

Jeremy tried not to show his emotional discomfort through the rest of the game. Neither of them stood to join in with the seventh inning stretch. By the end of the game, Judy and Jeremy were sitting separated, still sharing parts of the blanket for warmth.

"How's your jaw?" Judy asked as they walked home from the game.

"Seems to be getting a little stiffer as the night goes on." Jeremy moved his mouth trying to stretch the muscle of his jaw. "It will probably feel worse tomorrow."

"Aww, did he really hit you that hard?" Judy asked in concern.

"No, I was hoping for a sympathy kiss," Jeremy attempted at humor as they reached Judy's door.

"Oh, well, in that case," Judy smiled as she kissed his cheek.

"Thank you," Jeremy whispered.

"You're very welcome," Judy said lowering back to her feet.

"No," he stared intently into her eyes. "Thank you."

"For what?" Judy asked.

"For always being there for me. For showing how much you care," Jeremy mumbled.

Judy smiled and kissed his chin, "Get out of your head and just smile."

"Good night sweet Judy," he said with a smile and flourish.

Judy laughed, "Good night."

They found each other welcoming the embrace that followed and the brush of their lips against each other more urgently than either had expected. There was a shared reluctance when they parted.

"The good thing is that there are no more home games, so hopefully our dates won't be so…" Jeremy said searching for the word.

"Crazy?" supplied Judy.

"Good word," Jeremy said.

"Good night Jeremy," Judy said softly, and Jeremy almost thought he saw sadness in her eyes.

"Good night," he said again.

-SEVENTEEN-

Campus emptied almost entirely during the spring and summer terms. Most students either went home or were off working and avoiding campus, with the reminders of new semesters looming around the corner. The spring and summer terms were half the length of a semester, so class availability was limited. Jeremy decided to only take two classes during the spring, while Judy insisted on working straight through, as though it was a normal semester.

Whenever Judy was in class, Jeremy was training. His body changed by following the strict regime designed by Richards. The lower back pain from high school sports did not hurt as often anymore, because of all the extra stretching and exercises. Jeremy only pitched for a half hour each day to keep his arms loose. All of his real pitching practices were on Saturdays with Richards. During the week, Jeremy was instructed to do other activities to strengthen his arms.

Jeremy had always been plagued with the depth of his own mind. Judy was always telling him to get out of his head. He would harp on one thought and let his mind spiral downward. He doubted whether he was making Judy happy; he doubted if he could make it through the rest of the training. He especially doubted whether he had made the right decisions with regard to Steve.

Jeremy doubted that he would ever be able to understand why Steve had treated them the way he had this whole year. Had it all been a lie? What room did Steve have for being angry about him and Judy dating? He had had plenty of time to ask Judy out for himself, but, Jeremy thought, Judy had admitted that she had been attracted to Jeremy and not Steve, from the beginning. Steve probably recognized that she felt this way, even if Jeremy hadn't clued into it. No matter what Jeremy thought, he always felt like he had betrayed Steve. His doubts were even keeping him from being fully open with Judy. Their first day truly together had been blissful and too good to be true; like something from a fairy tale. Jeremy kept himself more reserved when around her, to test how she was taking Steve's revelation.

Judy didn't seem to be as bothered by the situation as Jeremy. She was definitely a different person than who he had first met last June. He was certain that not only did he like this new Judy, he knew she had unlocked the beginnings of a better version of himself. Jeremy kicked at the dirt of the mound on a hot, early summer morning, thinking about how soft he had become. His thoughts throughout a typical day bounced between Judy, school, training, and Judy again. It was hard to focus on anything or nothing. Sometimes, he felt that his head was trying to think about so many things at once that there was a head on collision of thoughts in his brain, and it would shut off entirely, leaving a horrible void, a vacuum desperately seeking something to fill the space. Then, the doubts would viciously take over.

"Man, summers here do get hot," Jeremy said removing his hat and wiping his forehead like he had seen so many pitchers do on television growing up. "I can't get over how quickly it heats up in the morning."

"We do live in what is considered a desert," Richards replied, tossing the ball back to Jeremy. "Just stay hydrated, or this will all be a waste."

"You don't have to tell me that twice," Jeremy said bending to catch up the water jug next to the mound. "I thought I wouldn't get so tired after I got into a routine of working out more consistently."

"The heat can do that to you," Richards admitted, slapping his glove to get Jeremy to get ready again.

"It sure can," Jeremy said before pitching again to Richards. This continued for another few minutes before Jeremy's pitches started getting sloppy with fatigue and Richards waved for a break.

As they walked over to the shade, Richards asked, "How is everything else going outside of practice?"

"Good. I can't complain," Jeremy sighed as he sat on the bench. "I've got three classes next term and we're already half way through this term."

"Does it give you enough variation in the day?" Richards asked, dumping large mouthfuls of water into his own mouth and removing his hat. His graying hair plastered to his head while the ends that had been free of the hat fanned out.

"It does." Jeremy swallowed. "Just enough work to keep me busy while not ruling my life."

"How is Judy?" Richards asked. "Is she distracting you from your goal?" he teased.

"Never," Jeremy chuckled. "She's been pushing me to do this from the beginning and been my one support outside of your coaching."

"Good. I hate to see it when one of my projects gets distracted along the way," Richards scowled.

"I don't think that will happen," Jeremy said. "We complement each other, which is probably for the best. We just fit," he sighed. At

Richards' continued scowl, he said hastily, "I'm trying not to get too distracted. It helps to have a little break from school and training. And, like I said, she was the one to push me into this when I was hesitating about trying out."

"What about the other issue?" Richards asked after a silent minute.

"Steve?" Jeremy confirmed. "Haven't seen him much. Judy is taking more classes to get ahead in school than I am, and she said that she sees him around once in a while, but I have no idea if they talk."

"I'm just relieved you didn't slug him back," Richards exhaled. "You have to keep those hands safe."

"Oh, I know," Jeremy said looking at his hands. "There were two things going through my head that stopped me."

"And what was that?" Richards asked.

"One, I didn't want to mess up my hand and live up to Steve's expectations," Jeremy admitted. "And two, I had just started dating Judy. I didn't want to do something stupid at the beginning that would make me lose her."

"Smart thinking," Richards smiled. "The whole situation is childish," Richards said.

"I know, I don't know what else I could have done to make it better," said Jeremy.

"Just don't let it get in your head. We've got enough to worry about if we are going to get you ready for tryouts."

"Agreed," Jeremy said promptly.

"I figure it's about time for you to have this," Richard said pulling something out of his duffle. "I know it's old, but it should do for a start."

Jeremy accepted the old glove from Richards. "Thanks, but I have a glove," he said questioningly.

Smiling, Richards simply said, "Look closer."

Jeremy examined the glove and his eyes lit up. It was a left handed pitching mitt. "Thanks! This will come in handy when you start teaching me with the left hand."

"Which is right about now if you're done being a sissy in the shade," Richards joked.

"A sissy eh?" Jeremy raised an eyebrow.

"I didn't stutter," came the reply over his shoulder as he walked out to the mound. "No more girl talk. It's hard labor for you."

"Yes sir," Jeremy smiled and ran up to the mound. "So, where did the glove come from?"

"It was mine," Richards said.

"Yours?" puzzled Jeremy.

"Yep. When I was younger than you I pitched left," Richards smiled.

Surprised, Jeremy said, "You did? You mean you don't anymore? I thought you pitched right."

"No, I don't do it anymore. I had an accident and couldn't throw left anymore," Richards explained flexing his left hand.

"So you switched to the right?"

"I had to. I couldn't give up the game, so I had to learn how to pitch right handed," he sighed. "I was never as good on my right, but it got me through high school and into college. Now I coach right handed, and you are one of the first in a long time I've admitted to that I was originally a southpaw."

"Wow, I admit, I wondered how you were going to be able to teach correctly how to throw left," Jeremy admitted.

"Doubting the teacher?" Richards stared.

"Not anymore," chuckled Jeremy in awe.

"I must admit," Richards said, "this experiment with you has been exciting for me. I'm sort of reliving a part of me that I thought was dead."

"Well, I'm excited to finally learn the left side," Jeremy said.

"Good, maybe now you'll stop whining about learning," he

smiled.

"I don't whine," muttered Jeremy.

Richards cleared his throat and Jeremy knew it was back to business. "Now, a thing you have to remember is that southpaws always look funny when they throw. It's weird, I know, but they just do."

"Probably because we are all so used to seeing right handed throws," offered Jeremy.

"Honestly, I haven't given it serious thought," Richards grunted.

"Right, sorry," Jeremy mumbled.

"May I continue?" Richards asked. Jeremy nodded. "Okay, we will be able to see how well you stuck to the workout routine I gave you and how well you can adapt what I've taught you."

While Richards ran back to home plate, Jeremy slipped on the lefty pitcher's mitt. He kept wanting to hold the ball with his right hand and was fighting the urge to face third base. Jeremy stood silently, looking down his right shoulder at Richards, and waged a mental war with his right leg to move. Finally, spastically, he raised and stepped out with his right leg and lobbed the ball with his left.

"Sorry," he called to Richards who was chasing the ball.

"Don't worry," Richards yelled back. "At least you got the correct leg to move."

"Yeah, at least," grumbled Jeremy.

"It'll come. Don't worry about fancy pitches. Let's just get your arm trained at pitching," Richards encouraged.

Jeremy nodded in agreement and started to settle into what he could assume was a mirror image of his right side technique. Internally, Jeremy tried to envision a mirror image of Richards pitching as though it was his left hand. Trying to focus more on how it should feel rather than the specifics in the pitch, Jeremy swung his right leg up and stepped out. His left arm did feel weird as it whirled to throw the ball. With each pitch, Jeremy felt slightly more confident. Had he not received the instruction over the last few months from Richards, pitching left handed would have been discouraging, especially since his left arm didn't move the same way his right did. Utilizing his entire body compensated for the awkwardness of throwing left.

After a number of pitches, Jeremy's body ached with each movement. His right was not getting any relaxation while putting his left through such extreme conditioning. Sweat was pouring down his face in the heat and exertion. Jeremy's breathing was more labored than when he swam. He was panting as his fingers traced the stitches of the ball. Deciding to force out all of his exhaustion in one last pitch, Jeremy switched his grip from a fastball, to the unpracticed curve.

"Where did that come from?" Richards asked as he caught the curveball.

"I thought I would push myself a bit," Jeremy said, walking to meet Richards. "I think I pushed it too hard," he said rubbing his left elbow.

"So you meant to throw a curve?" Richards raised an eyebrow.

"Yes, but I didn't expect it would hurt that much." Jeremy winced.

"It is one of those that will hurt a bit. There's more to the technique than what you delivered, but not bad for the first try," Richards congratulated. "We don't want to screw that shoulder and elbow up too soon. This is going to be your ticket in son," he said slapping both of Jeremy's shoulders with his glove. "This is what we need to 'wow' the coaching staff. You've got to be better than the average pitcher. You need to be great and then switch arms to show that you are just as good if not better on the other arm."

"At least this shoulder doesn't cramp up on me," Jeremy groused motioning to his left.

"Well, it still could. It's only the first day so don't bank on that just yet," Richards warned.

"It doesn't hurt to hope though," Jeremy reasoned tiredly.

LIFE, LOVE, AND BASEBALL

"You can do more than that," Richards replied seriously. "Keep up with what I've taught you on both arms and you should be fine."

"Ready for a few more?" Jeremy asked looking back at the mound.

"Let's not push it today," Richards said taking in Jeremy's exhaustion. Jeremy was silently rejoicing that the practice was over, but had wanted to sound enthusiastic. "We've still got to polish your style. Let's stop until next week, and you keep working on strengthening both arms."

"Are we only going to focus on pitching left for the next few weeks?" asked Jeremy curious.

"Absolutely not. You need to be perfect in both hands," Richards said fiercely. "Practices from here on out are going to be harder, because we will be increasing the demands on your body." Richards slammed both hands on Jeremy's shoulders for emphasis despite Jeremy wincing. "We have to get your body ready for the burn in both arms from full games of pitching. You have to be able to switch as needed, to respond to the hitter instead of responding to the pain. You have to throw through the pain when you want to switch arms. You have to be whatever type of pitcher the coach needs each pitch."

He paused and studied Jeremy. "We have a lot of work yet to do."

-EIGHTEEN-

Later that day, Jeremy was sitting on the couch with Judy next to him. He was adjusting ice packs while a summer afternoon MLB game played on the television. On his lap he had an old library book with a frame by frame series of photographs of a pitcher. On the arm of the couch, Jeremy had placed a printout of himself pitching recently in almost as many frames.

"You really do think a lot about baseball," Judy said without raising her eyes from her book.

"I'm sorry," Jeremy said shuffling the papers and book to put them away.

"No, I don't think you are," Judy said in a hard to read way.

"Are you upset with me?" Jeremy asked, trying to keep the fatigue from his voice.

"No, I know this must be hard work to make up for years of not playing. But," she said putting her book down. "I am your girlfriend now. So, let's act like we are dating a bit more and not just hang out on a couch."

"You're right," Jeremy said, laying the book and papers off to the side. "I'm sorry. It is hard work and I'm willing to do it, but I can't ice my arms while going out somewhere with you."

"I'm not asking you to do that," and she moved to look closely at him so he could see that she wasn't angry with him. "I'm just saying, when you are with me, be here with me."

"You're right," Jeremy exhaled. "My arm has had all the ice it can take right now anyway." He peeled off the athletic wrap holding the pack to his shoulders. "What do you want to do tonight?"

"Glad you asked," perked Judy. "There's a new movie I've wanted to see."

"Right," Jeremy said with a mock reluctance in his voice.

"Hey! We're not just friends anymore Jeremy," she teased with a stern voice. "You are my boyfriend, so you have to do these things with me if I have to watch you rip your arms off your shoulders."

"Fair enough. Let me go change my shirt," Jeremy said.

"Oh, can I watch?" she asked teasingly.

"Ha ha," Jeremy faked.

The movie ended up being almost entirely a waste of film. They were able to spend time together without homework or baseball, which they enjoyed. The time in the dark was spent holding hands with Judy's body turned towards Jeremy. She casually rested a leg on his and snuggled into him as though he were nothing more than a large teddy bear.

"Sorry that it wasn't a real date," Jeremy apologized as they left the theatre.

"The movie was decent, not horrible at least," she said when Jeremy snorted. "But, you should ask me out on a proper date sometime."

"I bet you'd like that wouldn't you?" Jeremy teased.

"Yep," She smiled. "Just ask me some other time, so I can be surprised."

"You are taking all the fun out of this by telling me how to do things," he smiled and poked her side.

"Well, I thought you needed the help. You are turning into a dumb jock," she said, poking him back.

"What does that make you?" he sneered.

"The smart, sexy, attractive, loyal girlfriend dating the dumb jock," she said without missing a beat.

"Like that ever happens in real life," Jeremy muttered.

"Good point," she said pretending to pout. "Okay, you're not a dumb jock."

"I didn't think so," Jeremy smiled. "But you are everything you said you were."

"Now you're just trying to butter me up," she pouted. "It doesn't work if I fed you the line."

He gave her a better line: a kiss.

Jeremy returned her to her door that night with a kiss on the top of her head while holding her close. "Good night Judy," he whispered into her hair.

"Good night," she said as she turned to go inside. "Oh, Jeremy?" she asked.

He stopped and turned back to her; "yes?"

"My parents are coming out here from Colorado in two weeks," she said nervously.

"What were they doing in Colorado?" Jeremy asked.

"That's where they live," Judy said.

"I thought they lived just a few hours north of us," Jeremy said, confused.

"They did when you and I met a year ago, but they moved to Colorado three months ago," she explained. "My little sister will be a freshman here, so they are bringing her out to college."

"So, you'd like me to be normal and not embarrass you. I under-stand and will stay out of the way. It's for the best," Jeremy joked.

"No! I want them to meet you," Judy implored.

"Thanks, I figured that one out on my own," Jeremy said holding her hands in reassurance.

"So, um… I hope that's not weird," Judy said.

"Oh, it's extremely…awkward and nerve racking, but that's part of the game," he said with a smile.

"Always a game eh?" she teased.

"Good night," Jeremy said, kissing her again.

Jeremy felt it was sappy to admit that he always felt empty after saying goodnight to Judy, but he could no longer deny how he felt. Jeremy's freshman year of college had been like most students. He moved around the different circles trying to find where he fit in. He didn't tie himself down to any group in particular, because he wanted to keep his options open; this was his new start after all.

After the summer term of his freshman year ended, Jeremy started to buckle down on real college life. He was required to attend his classes, like any serious student who wanted to make the most of tuition. Jeremy had started school later than most, after spending time after high school working to earn money for college. He had originally thought he would have to work for up to three years before applying, but he got a grant to come early. He worked hard his first year of school, and now he had a small scholarship to pay most of his tuition.

Being able to attend summer and spring terms helped him catch up for missed time. He met Steve and Judy at the beginning of his sophomore year. Now, a year later, he was almost finished with his sophomore credits. Judy had passed him in the extra classes she took and would be a good way into her junior year once summer term was over.

After two years of college, Jeremy had only one regret. It was a regret he never thought he would have. He regretted not being more interested with dating in high school and his freshman year of college. He was constantly worried about how he was treating Judy. Was he giving her enough attention? Was he smothering her? Did he say things the right way or was Judy just an extremely patient person? These were never questions he had felt before.

Though it was late, Jeremy had no interest in sleeping. His head kept whirling with questions. He climbed into his old Eagle, which he rarely used on campus. The ignition did not like to turn over. When it finally sputtered to life, the car would stall and die after backing up a few feet. No matter how much Jeremy had used the car when he first got it, the car liked to die at random intervals. Though it was an automatic, Jeremy got in the habit of driving with both feet. At stop lights, Jeremy would have to use his left foot for the break and his right still applying pressure on the accelerator to keep the RPMs up or the car would die. Driving in the hills at the bottom of the mountains was even more of an adventure.

Like a sleeping goblin, the car chugged along. They had already used the vehicle that night to get to and from the theatre, so it should have been warmed up, but it clearly would rather slumber in the dark parking lot of the apartment complex and lazily drool oil on the cement, angering the landlord.

There were a few places Jeremy liked to visit when he couldn't sleep at night and desperately craved a night drive. His first choice was always to head into the canyon. The canyon bent just enough that Jeremy didn't have to go very far before he could no longer see the light pollution. If he turned off the highway splitting the mountains and followed the winding paths up the face, he could really feel miles away from civilization.

He avoided the turn off that would lead him to the ski resort that ran year round as a getaway even without snow and stayed on the roads that would lead him deeper into the mountain woods. If he followed the road just long enough, he would pass the usual hotspots for late night dates, campfires, and anything else college couples did in these areas. He would finally come across a spot where he could safely park his car and not obstruct the narrow, winding, mountain road.

Jeremy remembered to turn off the cabin light of his car before opening his door after turning off the engine. He had the slightest concern that his car may not start again every time he stopped up in the mountains. Luckily, the mountain road was almost entirely a decline which could always help kick start the engine. He was even more lucky that he'd never had to attempt such a desperately stupid act.

Without the cabin light turning on when he opened the door, Jeremy's eyes were able to focus quickly on his surroundings. He loved coming up here at night. Even with so many aspen trees around him, the slightest sliver of a moon was all the light he needed to walk around. He'd pass the trees with the no trespassing signs and continue walking up the mountain as stealthily as possible.

Jeremy remembered the camping trips he had had as a boy with his father. They had lived in what was once called the Ohio Territory. His father admired the Native Americans, who had created the beautiful history of the Ohio valley. Every hike with his brothers and father turned into a lesson of supposed Native American tracking skills; not being an expert on such skills, Jeremy suspected that they had simply been his father's interpretation on how an earth-respecting person would move through the woods. They would not rush along the trails. Instead, they made each movement deliberate and as limited as required. Their goal was to be trackless. They had to be able to walk through the woods and not disturb the natural order of life. You didn't move a low hanging branch. You respected the limb and walked or crawled under it so as to not disturb its slumber. His father loved to have them hang back from the rest of the scout troop and then see if Jeremy could find them. There was always someone who brushed past the ferns too closely and bent the life. Despite the efforts of the leaders, someone always stabbed at a tree with their pocket knife. Eventually, they became so talented with moving through the woods silently, that everyone wanted Jeremy and his brothers on their team at night when they played capture the flag around the campsite.

Jeremy didn't have any qualms about wandering off the path and into private property. He knew it was disrespectful to laws, but he took care to leave little trace of where he went. He was willing to follow the natural lay of the land, even if it lead him in a roundabout course before finally sending him to where he wanted to go. He never told anyone where he went and had not yet been caught. While he was no longer in the practice of silently moving through the woods, Jeremy still approached every step with respect.

After a few more minutes, Jeremy reached the clearing he had come to visit. He always stopped and waited, as though seeking the permission of the clearing before entering. As if it was sacred ground, Jeremy would bow his head, remove his shoes, pull out the canvas-over shoes he had made and left in the trunk and slowly walk into the clearing. Each step was slow and deliberate. He tested his weight with each step to make sure he was not stepping on something that would break. The canvas-over shoes gave just enough protection while allowing feeling through his feet.

Jeremy never went to a pre-determined spot in the clearing. His slow progress allowed him to imagine he was feeling the breath of the forest, listening for when it told him to stop. Always fighting the urge to lay down in the field, Jeremy would stop and stand perfectly still. Occasionally, he would crouch in the tall grass and hope to see some form of life at night.

Even with the many sounds of the forest at night, Jeremy found it more peacefully silent than being enclosed in a quiet room. The sounds of the forest belonged here and added to the sacredness of this spot. Jeremy never brought anyone here, because he felt that the sanctity of this spot would be tainted. Here, Jeremy would kneel and open his soul. The most damage he deliberately made to this location was when he dug his fingers into the mountain soil; imagining his pain draining through his fingers. The mountain was constant and firm and could withstand any pain he shared.

Jeremy always felt like a vastly different person when he visited this spot. Any time he came into the mountains, he felt like a part of his being woke up, but this spot, in particular, he only visited when in special need of support. He could talk himself and find reason in the chaos. He words seemed so out of place in the forest that he instantly realized how pathetic and childish his fears had become.

He wondered vaguely, if the understanding he and his father had over the ancients who inhabited the earth before them, was even correct. Was the earth a sleeping being? Was it wise and noble and containing secrets of knowledge? Whatever the case may be, when Jeremy left, he thanked the clearing for keeping him safe before returning to the car.

Driving back down the mountain was often a depressing situation; it signaled a return to the pressures he faced. Jeremy felt hope that he wasn't entirely alone. Jeremy never had many friends growing up. He usually maintained a few close friends for a while. Then, something usually happened that would abruptly end the friendship. Usually it was something as simple as someone moving or a change in interests. Jeremy noted how blessed he was to have Judy supporting him in his dream to try out for the baseball team. He even mentally thanked the friendship he was making with Richards throughout the training. Both Richards and Judy helped Jeremy get through each day.

Steve was right about Jeremy, he admitted as he drove down the mountain. Jeremy was a bit self-centered. He could get so moody and depressed if he stuck inside his head for too long. He drained Judy and Richards of all the support they had for him. Jeremy hadn't even let his parents know that he was trying out for the team. He couldn't even explain why he hadn't told them.

Jeremy realized, for the first time, that he was a walking hypocrisy in nearly every aspect of his life. He craved the attention of people close to him and yet shut them out. He needed support on his dreams but wouldn't even share those dreams with his parents or family. He wanted to keep Steve as a friend but chose the path that drove Steve away. This was what Jeremy finally realized was scaring him about dating Judy. He didn't want his hypocrisy to hurt her in any way, because he was too hesitant to make the right decision. He was getting too old to be acting so childish and indecisive. He liked Judy. His feelings for her grew each day. He was having a harder time staying focused on working toward making it to the tryouts. He still could not figure out what he wanted to do for a career.

Jeremy rested his head against the steering wheel in the parking lot of his apartment. He was completely exhausted. He had the tendency to fall into a slump when he let himself get so tired. Add on top of that, being alone late at night. Could he measure up to what Judy wanted her parents to see in him? He turned the struggling car off and got out. He locked the door and walked to his apartment. His roommates appeared to be either asleep or had gone home for the weekend. He grabbed a drink of water from the kitchen, sitting on the couch. Judy had left her book again on his couch. He was surprised she hadn't texted him to see if she could get it from him; he knew she liked to read in bed before falling asleep.

Jeremy stood up and quickly got ready for bed before turning out all the lights in the apartment. His roommate had gone home for the weekend, so Jeremy didn't feel bad about turning the light on to get ready for bed. He pulled out his netbook, turned off the light and crawled into his bed.

Flipping open the cover of the netbook, he checked his email, news feeds, and then turned on a movie. The little computer warmed on his chest through the sheet, as it slowly rose and fell with his breathing. Jeremy didn't really pay attention to the movie, because he knew it by heart. It was one of his favorite baseball movies. The typical story he himself was trying to live of chasing a dream despite numerous obstacles and hopefully win the girl along the way. Jeremy chuckled and thought that despite the similarities his story would never be movie material. He was already with Judy and, at the moment, if he didn't make it to tryouts, he would still be happy.

-NINETEEN-

"Are you nervous about meeting her parents?" Richards was asking the week before they would come.

"Only when I'm not practicing or training," Jeremy said, tossing the ball back to Richards as they warmed up.

Chuckling, Richards said, "Gee that leaves a fair amount of the day."

"You're telling me," Jeremy frowned while shaking out his arms.

"Well, hopefully this will keep them off your mind for the morning," Richards prefaced. "Next week is the last week of the intramurals right?" Richards asked.

"The softball season ended. I've also been playing in the fast pitch short league," Jeremy replied.

"Are you going to try pitching?" asked Richards.

"I never really pitched in the first place," Jeremy said. "There were only a few times when I pitched, and it was before you came along."

"Are you going to try to pitch at this game though?" Richards asked.

"Do you think that I should?" Jeremy was uncertain.

"It would be a good experience for you," Richards scratched his chin. "We are getting closer, every day, to tryouts. The heat is really going to kick in,"

"Great, right as the summer comes into full season as well," Jeremy grumbled while gulping water.

"Don't wimp out on me now," Richard said sternly.

"I'm not," Jeremy said defensively. "I'm too close to give up now."

"That's what I'd rather hear. Let's get going then," Richards said, slapping Jeremy on the shoulders.

Pitching practice continued almost as usual. Richards was more willing to instruct Jeremy on how to throw curves, sliders, two seam fastballs, as well as how to work with the signals used most often to signify which pitch to throw. Jeremy quickly learned how to deal with this new type of fatigue; the kind that results from strenuous and correct practicing. He had been worked to breaking point in different sports.

In pitching, he found a different fatigue from repeating the same movements with only minute variation. It was different than soccer or even wrestling. Even if you performed the same drill in wrestling, there was always something different that could happen, because you always had to go against someone else. Now, it was just Jeremy and Richards. There was no real variation in possible outcomes, other than how well Jeremy could pitch, his focus, and the fatigue creeping steadily into his arm.

He fought to keep his mind focused. The pitches were blurring themselves together. All the next week, Jeremy felt as though he was pitching. He had talked to the team captain about pitching, and it was agreed that Jeremy would be able to start the game and see how far he could go.

The first inning went well for Jeremy. He kept it slow and simple.

He didn't really want to have to show anything with his left arm yet; his confidence was shaky on the left. Jeremy started the game, concerned about how well he would do just pitching with his right. He had been feeling comfortable over the last few weeks when it was only him and Richards. Now, all he wanted to do was vomit.

At the bottom of the second inning, Jeremy's team, representing the home team, returned to the dugout. As he did so, Jeremy could see that Judy and her family had arrived. Judy waved him over to meet her family, because he wouldn't be hitting during the game.

"You must be Judy's parents," Jeremy said, wiping his hands off on a towel from his gym bag. "Sorry that we are meeting for the first time here and that I'm not more presentable."

"That's alright," Judy's father said. "We like sports in our family," he said while shaking hands with Jeremy.

"Judith tells us you are the pitcher?" Judy's mother asked in confirmation.

"Well, trying to be one at least. Today's the first time officially," Jeremy explained.

"Jeremy's going to try out for the team," Judy stated aloud, though it seemed that she had already told her family this news.

"Did you play going up," her father asked.

"No," Steve said interrupting as he walked up. "But, he's got this idea that he can make the team if he tries hard enough," he said offering his hand. "I'm Steve, a friend of these two," Steve offered, despite the glance between Jeremy and Judy.

"I'm sorry?" Judy's mother said. "What do you mean?"

"Well, as Jeremy has no real experience," Steve started with emphasis on the lack of experience. "He is trying to learn how to pitch with either hand as his edge for why the coaches should consider him."

"That's ambitious," Judy's father said with raised eyebrows.

"It's crazy, that's what it is," Steve sneered. "Crazy and stupid."

"I'll admit that it is a bit crazy," Jeremy said, trying to stay calm while glancing over everyone to see how the inning was progressing and rubbing his shoulder. "I ran into a guy who's been helping me out during the week."

Steve laughs, "Yeah, he's a little league coach."

Judy's sister giggled at this. Judy's mother asked, "You must be joking."

"Well, not too far off actually," Jeremy said, clearing his throat. "He coaches a youth league. He has a lot of experience with the schools around here, with training their pitchers. He saw me throwing one morning and has been working with me ever since."

"He's actually getting really good," Judy said beaming and refusing to look at Steve.

"Right," Steve said, waving to a fellow teammate. "If you'll excuse me, the top of the inning is almost up and I'll be batting next," Steve said beginning to move away. "It was nice to meet you," he said looking at Judy's parents. "Stick around and I'll show you a real ballplayer."

"Charming young man Judith," her father said skeptically.

"Well, we're actually not the best of friends as of late," Judy said sadly.

"Yeah, personally I think that the falling out was because he had something for your daughter and was upset when Judy and I finally got together."

"Is that true?" her mother asked excitedly.

"That's not the whole reason," Judy supplied.

"I think it is more than what we give him credit for," Jeremy said. He let the statement hang and walked Judy's family to find some seats in the few bleachers around the diamond. Jeremy excused himself so he could go stay lose with his catcher while his team finished up the bottom of the inning.

Pitching became more complicated for Jeremy; he was keenly

aware of at least three very interested pairs of eyes watching how he did. At the close of the inning, Jeremy walked back with his team and tipped his hat at the wave from Judy and her mother. Off to the side of the bleachers, and in a camp chair, Richards sat grinning with a notebook, camera, and a can of lemonade. Jeremy jogged over to his pro-bono coach.

"How's the game?" Richards asked when Jeremy was within earshot.

"What are you doing here?" Jeremy asked surprised?

"I wanted to see how you are doing under pressure," Richards smiled.

"I'm okay," Jeremy shrugged. "It's the middle of the fourth inning and my arm feels fine."

"Pitched any with your left yet?" Richards asked.

"No. I didn't think that you would want me to do that yet," Jeremy said.

"Glad to see you are listening to your coach," smiled Richards.

"I am. Uh, since you are here," Jeremy said shiftily. "You can meet Judy and her parents."

"I'd love too," Richards smiled and he stood up from his chair to gather his belongings with Jeremy's help.

"Judy, uh, everybody?" Jeremy said looking first at Judy and then her parents and sister. "I'd like you to meet my personal coach, Mr. Richards."

"Nice to meet you Mr. Richards," Judy's father said, the first to get up.

"It's Adam," Richards said.

"George," Judy's father said. "This is Martha and our daughters Judith and Sarah," he said motioning to each in turn.

"How do you do?" Adam Richards said shaking hands.

Jeremy heard the bottom of the fourth end and said, "You'll have to excuse me. I've got to run."

"Go on. Your team needs you," George said.

"This is exciting!" Martha bubbled.

"Good luck," Judy called, knowing that Jeremy was seriously struggling with his nerves at this point.

"Keep it relaxed," Richards called sternly in warning.

Jeremy nodded as he jogged back to the mound. Between the few warm-up pitches he had before the first batter of the inning, Jeremy glanced over to see that Richards had been invited to sit with Judy and her family in the bleachers. Judy and her mother waved to Jeremy again as he went back to warming up. He could see Steve with his team in the dugout sourly watching Judy and her family.

Pitching became harder to focus on throughout the next few innings. His hand felt like it was buzzing in the strain. Steve's large team lineup made it so he didn't come up to bat again until later in the game. That didn't stop Steve from catcalling Jeremy when his focus and strength began to slip.

"You're going to have to do better than that to stop us from winning this game," Steve yelled even though his team was behind by two runs.

"Shut up Steve," Jeremy said to himself. Still, it must have shown how much it burned Jeremy when he made stupid mistakes. He should have known to expect that this wouldn't have been the best experience as far as his pitching record was concerned.

Immediately following the next pitch, as though he hadn't really been paying attention to the outcome or quality and just wanted to be insulting, Steve yelled, "Still not good enough for the college team. Why don't you just settle for us lowly mortals?" Surprisingly, his team found this particular catcall to be humorous.

Softly whispering to himself without moving his lips, Jeremy said, "Just like a real game I guess. Thanks for the help Steve."

By the top of the seventh inning, Jeremy was really starting to hurt in his arm and, ashamed to admit, his pride. Steve had yelled at the top of his lungs, "Did you know the pitcher is going to try out for the college team? They must be really desperate to want a fool like that." Jeremy was only partly thankful for the handful of boos and hisses from his team in response to Steve.

"Give them a quick three!" he heard Judy yell as he reached the mound.

"Stay loose," Richards reassuring boom penetrated the field.

"Right," Jeremy said as his hand shook. "Relaxed and loose. Easier said than done." He let out the air, threw with all his remaining strength and was satisfied that it surprised even the members of Steve's team.

"Strike one!" the umpire called.

"Lucky pitch," Steve called. "His arm will give out soon if he tries to throw that fast again."

"Not likely," Richards said quietly to Judy's family, hoping that Jeremy felt this confident.

Jeremy surprised himself with the speed and accuracy of his next pitch.

"Strike two!" yelled the umpire.

"Is that one a lucky pitch as well?" one of Jeremy's teammates called from the field to Steve. The rest of the team and many people in the crowd, Judy's family included, chuckled.

Jeremy tried to stay focused again. His face fell into his familiar expression of concentration. He closed his eyes and focused on controlling his breathing. Adding to the mental image of a coiled spring, Jeremy added the force of his frustration with Steve. His leg drove up and forward as though with a mind of its own. His lips pulled back away from his grinding teeth as he released his arm to swing around and propel the small, white, missile from his hand. At the very last second Jeremy released the ball from his fingers in just the right way to give it a curve.

The ball sped through the air and dipped at the last moment, out of the reach of the swinging bat.

"Strike three!" the Umpire pumped the air with emphasis while the catcher shook out his hand from his glove.

"I bet that's a third-time's-the-charm or something right?" the catcher yelled at Steve, massaging his hand.

"Next batter!" the Umpired yelled nervously. "Keep it friendly!"

Jeremy smiled as he caught Judy and her family cheering from the corner of his eye. He couldn't help but notice as well that Richards was stone faced while watching Jeremy. Knowing what Richards was most likely thinking, Jeremy checked his next throw and eased up on the types of pitches he was throwing.

By the beginning of the bottom of the seventh inning, the score was tied. Jeremy's team was determined to increase the lead before the start of the ninth inning. The bases were nearly loaded when the first batter struck out. The next batter fouled out, but the runners stole third and second. Finally, they were able to bring in the runners on second and third to lead the game by two.

At the beginning of the eighth inning, Jeremy noticed how sluggish his arm felt as he warmed up with the catcher. He would probably have to get someone else to pitch if he wasn't willing to pitch with his left arm. This was the final game of the fast pitch season, and his team would be the champions if they won. Jeremy was not sure he was willing to risk the game by trying his left arm out against opponents just yet.

"Strike one!" the umpire grunted for the first batter of the eighth inning. Jeremy was not pleased to see how sloppy his pitches were becoming.

The next pitch was a foul ball. "Got lucky on that one!" Steve yelled.

"I know that," Jeremy muttered to himself. "Just shut up and watch this one."

Jeremy threw as hard as he could, throwing his entire body in to the pitch. He grunted in the resultant pain and had to take it easy for the rest of the inning. The batters were hit out. The first batter was thrown out at first. The next two had pop flies that resulted in outs two and three. Jeremy tried to avoid Richards glare as he walked back to the dugout, hoping to rest his arm before the last inning.

Every pitch at the beginning of the ninth inning sent excruciating pain from shoulder to finger tips. Jeremy was pridefully desperate to finish the inning. His team still held the lead at two runs and would win if he could just strike out this inning without any runs scored. He doubted he could make it when one pitch went completely wild as Jeremy fought back the urge to cry out in pain, but the batter's eye was poor, and he struck himself out. Jeremy's team supported him by cheering, but Jeremy saw Richards raise slightly from the bench, watching him intently.

Jeremy's left hand acted of its own accord and cradled the right. Richards, jogged out to the mound as Jeremy called for a time out.

"Oh, that's convenient," Steve sneered loudly. "His arm gives out now before I can go up against him."

"I'd like to pop him one in the mouth," grumbled Jeremy to Richards.

"So would I, and I'd let you if we could risk your hands, but, we can't," Richards said appraising Jeremy. "Can we hurt your pride a bit and stop?"

"You said I'd have to learn to pitch through the pain," Jeremy reasoned.

"I didn't mean now though," Richards said. "You're not ready. You don't have enough playing time yet."

"I'm ready enough for this," Jeremy argued.

"Are you the coach now?" Richards asked.

"I don't need to go full strength. Just enough for one more batter," Jeremy suggested.

"This game is not as important as the ultimate goal," Richards warned.

"This game is important to me," Jeremy insisted.

Steve yelled, "So, what's it going to be? Are you quitting? Or are you going to amaze us with this hidden talent of switch pitching?"

While Steve's team laughed, Jeremy asked, "What's the count?"

"This is the second batter," Richards said. "The count is three balls and 2 strikes. Strike him out and you only have one more batter."

By this point, the umpire had joined them at the mound. "Look guys," he said. "This is only an intramural game. It doesn't really matter this much."

"Games always matter," Jeremy said fiercely. "I need to finish this or I'll never be able to make it when it's time."

"I need to know what your plan is," the umpire said. "I'm just a volunteer. This is getting too heated for what I signed up for."

"Hey Ump!" one of Steve's teammates called. "How much longer are you going to let him stall like this?"

"We know he can't hack it," Steve encouraged his team.

In the stands, Judy's father was shaking his head in disgust. "No class," he murmured while Judy's mother patted his arm. Judy was stoically facing the commotion on the mound.

"Can you do one last batter?" goaded Steve. "I will bat against you, but you have to pitch with your left hand," he said, walking out to the mound with a bat to show his readiness. "If he's such a great pitcher, then prove it with his ability to pitch left handed as he has boasts."

"What are you talking about?" the umpire asked. "He hasn't said anything. Get back to your dugout."

"Why are you doing this Steve?" Jeremy asked.

"To prove before it's too late that you can't do this. That it won't work. That you are being a fool and have wasted your time, your friends' time, your teams' time, and this man's time," he said motioning to Richards.

"I'll be the judge of how my time is spent," Richards growled. "And as for his team, they are keeping your team at bay because of Jeremy. So, I'd say he hasn't been wasting his time at all."

"You're next?" Jeremy said. "I can strike this guy out and then strike out Steve. With my left hand."

"Jeremy," Richards started to warn.

"It's alright," Jeremy said. Then turning to Steve, "Get off my mound, and I warn you not to crowd my plate."

"I don't think this is a good idea," Richards said.

"Neither do I, but it is the test I need," Jeremy said stretching his left arm.

"Why do I have a bad feeling about this?" Richards asked Jeremy as Steve and the umpire left the mound.

Jeremy promised, "I won't go too hard, just hard enough to strike him out."

Richards nodded and left the field while Jeremy stretched. He finished off the current batter with his right and stretched his left arm out.

"Are you ready?" the umpire called to Jeremy who nodded. "Next batter," he called to Steve who sauntered up to the plate.

Jeremy had not brought the glove Richards gave him and had to borrow a left handed mitt from a team mate and returned to the mound. He failed to block the catcalls and booing from the other team out of his head. He also failed miserably at being able to soak in any encouragement from his own team. Jeremy wished he was allowed to have some practice pitches with his left hand. After pitching the entire game right handed, he was having trouble remembering the difference in his windup for throwing left.

Steve clipped the ball of the first pitch but to Jeremy's relief, it went foul.

"Foul ball!" the umpire called. "Strike one!"

"Oh, that's cheap!" Steve yelled as he readied his stance.

"I was being nice," Jeremy lied. "That's the closest you are going to get." Then he turned away from Steve and whispered to himself, "Relax, you need to control the pitch."

"It's a cheap strike," Steve complained.

"A cheap strike?" Jeremy whirled. "Fine. Ump? That was my warm up pitch. No strike."

"Um, I'm not sure we can do that," the umpire said tentatively.

"No, strike. Let's go," Jeremy insisted.

"Um, No Strike," the umpire called out. "Count is no balls, no strikes, and two outs."

"Come on hot shot," Steve yelled.

From in the stands, Judy was clutching her hands together in great anticipation and confusion. "What are they doing?" she asked without blinking.

"Being idiots," Richards groused.

"Why don't they count the strike?" asked Sarah, who until now had been disinterested with the proceedings.

"Because of their pride," Richards grumbled.

"Do you think he has the strikes in him?" George asked.

"We'll see," was all Richards could say.

Jeremy was again staring down his right shoulder. He was trying to envision that the park was empty and Richards was crouched at home plate. Instead, he felt an intense hatred for his once friend. Jeremy debated whether his decision to pitch left handed had been the proper move. Regardless, he was in this situation now and had to resolve it alone.

"Strike one!" the umpire called to Jeremy's profound relief.

Jeremy could hear his catcher yelling above the crowd, "That's one, and it counts."

"Shut up," muttered Steve.

"Come on Steve. Ram it back at him!" Steve's team rallied.

Jeremy wound up and delivered another awkward-feeling pitch. He was surprised when the umpire yelled, "Strike two!"

Judy was starting to release her fear to the excitement. She was conflicted; she didn't want Steve to be humiliated, but, she wanted Jeremy to succeed more than she wanted to protect Steve's pride or friendship. She dug her nails into the fabric around her legs and tried not to look at her family or Mr. Richards.

Emboldened by two successful strikes and the uncounted foul ball, Jeremy finally began to succeed in blocking out anyone else from his mind. He even began to force out the image of Judy cheering and congratulating him when the game would end.

Suddenly, as Jeremy nodded at the signal from the catcher, the world went silent. Jeremy felt that his body had taken over the movements. His lungs pushed out the air they held through his lips. His arms coiled up for the windup as his right leg rose from the ground. Coiling up, his lungs expanded to pull in another breath. There was the slightest pause at the peak of the windup as the coil begged to be released. Jeremy felt his leg shoot out to drive the coil. His breath came out in a surge as he stepped forward. His left arm seemed to be detached from his brain as it arced through the air. He had never felt this comfortable in pitching left handed. His weight shift and his left leg began to raise as the ball left his fingers. Jeremy hadn't even been able to tell his fingers or hand how to handle the release; his hand reacted of its own accord.

As his left leg swung around to finish the motion, Jeremy watched the ball through the air. It seemed to take forever and yet no time at all before the umpire yelled, "Strike three! You're out!" and he backed away from Steve fearing reprisal.

The volume was turned up as Steve pounded the plate. Jeremy hastily left the mound, returned the glove to his teammate, and nursed both arms; completely oblivious of the celebrations of his team for clinching the championship.

"What happened?" Richards scolded Jeremy.

"Nothing, it just stings a bit," Jeremy admitted, ashamed at giving into Steve.

"Where?" Richards demanded brusquely.

"Mainly at the elbow," Jeremy pointed. "My right hurts worse obviously."

Richards grabbed Jeremy's arms, bent them in various directions and speeds while prodding with his fingers. "Get out of here before anyone else talks you into something foolish," he said with the tiniest flicker of a grin at the corner of his eyes. "Ice that all night before it gets worse," he said point to Jeremy's right arm. "Seems like you over extended on too many of those pitches. We'll work on that next week. We may be able to avoid disaster yet," he said before storming off with his belongings.

Judy grabbed Jeremy's hand at that moment and extracted him from the gathering team. She led him quickly to her retreating family. "We have your sports bag," she said breathlessly. "I thought you might like to get a clean getaway. They will leave it by my car."

"Thank you," Jeremy sighed in relief and pain. He didn't have to turn around to know that someone was staring forlornly at his and Judy's retreating forms.

"I told my parents we would meet them for dinner," Judy said later as she pulled into the apartment parking.

"Okay," Jeremy said distantly.

"You were seriously great out there," Judy said softly.

"Yeah? At what cost," he replied bitingly.

"What's the matter?" she asked.

"I'm sorry. I shouldn't have gotten angry. I'm just frustrated," he apologized quickly.

"At what? You proved that what you have been doing is working," she offered.

"But, is it enough? Or have I pushed myself too far today and screwed everything up," he grimaced as he raised his arms in emphasis.

"Jeremy?" she said softly.

"Sorry," Jeremy looked away and put a hand on the handle of the car door.

"What is really bothering you?" she asked a little afraid of the answer.

"I'm just angry at Steve for insisting on proving me wrong," he sighed. "I'm mad at myself for letting him goad me into pitching left handed. I'm furious at the pain in my arms for going too hard to prove a point. I'm worried that Richards won't help me anymore. I'm worried that I screwed up my arms," he unloaded in a rush.

"I'm sure you'll be okay," Judy tried to be cheerful. "Just do what Mr. Richards said. Ice your elbow and shoulders. Maybe take something for the pain and come out with my family so they can properly meet you and forget about the stress for the night."

"Fine," Jeremy said opening the door. "I'll hurry or do you want me to catch up with you?"

"It's up to you," Judy said. "I'll wait if you want."

"No, that's okay." Jeremy thought out loud. "Go be with your family. I don't want to hold you up. I'll try to go fast."

"Okay. See you soon," Judy said and pulled away.

-TWENTY-

Jeremy thought that training had prepared his arms, but now, as Jeremy tried the simple task of remove his shirt, he wanted to cry. The pain burned in his arms and he mentally cursed himself again. Why had he been so stupid to fall into this trap? Was this Steve's intention? Goad him into making a fool of himself in front of Judy's family and ruin his arms? No, Steve may be jealous of Judy's affections and unsupportive of Jeremy's baseball dream, but he wasn't so conniving as to sabotage Jeremy's arms.

Jeremy was almost to his shower when he thought about taking an over the counter pain reliever. "Better to let it have longer to work," he muttered to himself.

The heat of the shower almost hurt as much as it soothed. Jeremy wanted to relax in the shower. However, there was the fear of leaving Judy and her family waiting beyond necessary; assuming that they would even approve of his presence once he finally showed up.

Gingerly, Jeremy finished his shower and dressed. He pulled himself into his car and made his way up town to the restaurant Judy had texted him while he was showering. An ice pack lay melting on his passenger seat as Jeremy tried to keep an athletic wrap from tangling around his feet and the peddles of his car.

Holding one end of the wrap in his mouth, Jeremy secured the ice pack to his elbow, as he had become more accustomed to the pain in his shoulder, while walking into the restaurant.

"Can I help you?" the host asked staring oddly at the ice pack on Jeremy's right elbow as he fastened the clasps to hold the wrap in place.

"Oh, it's nothing," Jeremy tried to pass off, nodding to his arm. "I'm supposed to meet a party," he started.

"Are you Jeremy, the pitcher?" asked a waitress smiling, having just joined Jeremy and the host.

"Uh, sure?" Jeremy said taken aback.

"There was a party I sat not a few minutes ago that told me to look for someone like you. They said you might have an ice pack on your arm. I'll take you to their table," she said leading him away into the restaurant.

"But, I'm not sure," he started in the bustle of the crowded restaurant. He found it odd that Judy or her family would describe him as a pitcher to a complete stranger, as though he was someone more valuable than he was.

"There's our star!" Judy's mother called as Jeremy and the waitress rounded the corner.

Judy spun in her seat to beam, red cheeked, at Jeremy, "You made it! We just sat down about five minutes ago." She kissed him on his cheek as he sat next to her. His cheeks burned, and he noticed the slight disgust on Sarah's face but wasn't able to catch her parents reaction.

"Nice job tonight son," George said approvingly.

"Uh, thanks," Jeremy said getting settled in his seat. "It was only an intramural game," he said bashfully.

"Still, it was very exciting," Martha beamed.

"To be honest," Jeremy swallowed. "That is not the way I would have wanted you to meet me for the first time."

"Oh, don't worry about it," twittered Martha waving off his concern as though it was housefly.

"Well, I do actually," Jeremy shrugged.

"How so?" George asked reaching for the appetizers that had just arrived.

"Well, I um," Jeremy swallowed again, painfully aware how open he was being and starting to feel warm. "You see," he swallowed again and took a quick sip of water. "Judy and I have been good friends since the end of our freshman year here. We just started dating a few months ago in April." He noticed that Judy's parents tensed a bit and realized too late that he shouldn't pause for so long. "So, she means a lot to me," stupid thing to say next. They'll surely be suspect a big announcement or question, he thought.

"She means a lot to us too," George cleared his throat.

"Right, uh... I just wanted you to not worry about her. I thought I would meet you all for the first time in a setting like this. Not at a baseball game."

"What's wrong with that?" Sarah asked while texting on her phone.

"What's wrong is that I was sweaty, dirty, and I let my pride get in the way. I wasn't my best self out there, and I'm sorry about that. It's not the impression I would have wanted to be the first."

Everyone was silent at the table for a few moments. George finally spoke. "Thank you," he said softly.

"Yes, that means a lot," Martha agreed warmly.

"What you did right now means more to us than you can imagine," George said. "Especially as you are dating our daughter."

"Again, I'm sorry," Jeremy started but was interrupted by George.

"It takes a lot of integrity to admit that you are human. Yeah, we all have our tempers. I'm not condoning allowing a temper as an excuse, but I know that I've lost mine a fair number of times," he said with a smile at Martha. Both Martha and Sarah snorted with laughter before they both buried themselves in their drinks.

"Be that as it may," he continued. "It really shows maturity that the first thing you did was man up to how you were and share with us that you wanted to give a better impression," he smiled. "But, honestly son, we've had a long drive, just relax."

"We can tell that you are a fine young man," Martha patted his hand. "We have seen how determined you are to do the right thing."

"Absolutely," George agreed setting down his glass. "Now, is there something you would like to ask us?"

"Dad!" Judy shrieked causing heads to turn in the restaurant.

"Wait? WHAT?" Jeremy said slowly catching on.

"Didn't you want us to meet him, because he was going to ask our permission to marry you?" Martha asked her stunned daughter.

"Whoa! Wait," Jeremy said getting hot around his collar. "I just. No you've. I'm not. You've got the wrong idea."

"Is she not good enough?" George asked and Jeremy missed his smile.

"No. I mean she is," Jeremy blundered. "I love," Judy's hand tightened on his arm, "being around her," he felt her hand relax hesitantly. "She's amazing."

"Mom, we're only dating," Judy insisted. "We spend a lot of time together and I've talked about him on the phone. You said you wanted to meet him. You initiated this," she said defensively.

"Oh, okay then," Martha said with a smile.

"Awkward," Sarah mumbled.

"You're telling me," Jeremy said before realizing he had done so out loud.

The entire table was completely silent and staring at Jeremy before they burst out laughing.

"All I can say is that I am so relieved you aren't like that jerk, whatever his name was," George said wiping his mouth. "The last batter you struck out."

"Steve," Judy and Jeremy said together.

After a pause George opened his menu. "We better decide on what to eat now that you are here son."

Promptly, Jeremy snatched his menu and buried his burning face behind it, but not before he could hear Martha and George chuckling.

"This is starting off great," Jeremy said through clenched teeth to Judy.

"You almost said those three little words," Judy teased.

"I paused because of your vice grip on my arm," Jeremy defended.

"Uh huh," Judy said unconvinced. "I think they like you."

"Is that a good thing?" Jeremy whispered. "I feel like they're sizing me up for dinner."

"Oh, they are," Judy nodded going back to her menu. "That's how Dad has fun."

"Thanks for the warning," Jeremy grumbled.

By the end of the evening, Jeremy was feeling properly drowsy from the pain relievers, the enormous amounts of food Martha's motherly instinct insisted he consume, and the relaxation from good company. Having discarded the melted bag of ice, Jeremy was fidgeting with the athletic wrap as the party walked out of the restaurant into a pleasant summer evening air.

"It was so very nice to meet you finally Jeremy," Martha was saying, walking arm-in-arm with Judy.

"Thank you," Jeremy said graciously. "It was a pleasure spending some time with you."

"You're a fine ballplayer and a good young man," George said extending hand.

"Thank you, sir," Jeremy shook his hand.

"Good night sweetie," Martha said, hugging Judy tightly.

"Good night," Judy said in return and kissed her parents on the cheek.

Jeremy and Judy walked to their respective cars while Judy's family melted into the darkness. Judy's hand found Jeremy's and he gave it an appreciative squeeze.

"That wasn't so bad was it?" Judy asked.

"Not at all," Jeremy said. "It was actually a lot of fun."

"You sound surprised," Judy teased.

"I only meant that because I am tired and in pain that I was surprised I enjoyed myself," Jeremy explained.

"Good, because both of my parents, separately, insisted I bring you up for the fourth of July weekend," Judy said with a smile.

"Whoa, that's a big step," Jeremy said surprised.

"I told you they liked you," Judy smiled proudly.

"Yeah, like to make me stress out," Jeremy moaned.

"I don't doubt that," Judy said as she reached up on her toes to kiss his cheek. "Go get some sleep," she whispered.

"I really did enjoy the night," Jeremy looked at her. "It was nice."

"I'm glad," Judy kissed him. "But, I won't keep you up. You look exhausted."

"I am."

"Are you going to be okay with driving home?" she asked with concern.

"Yes, I should be," Jeremy said unlocking his door. "Good night," he said before kissing her on the top of her head. With one last hug, they parted and drove home.

"This is why you are supposed to listen to me," Richards commented a week later.

Jeremy was struggling to maintain any form in his pitches. "I know, I'm sorry," he consented.

"Well, sorry isn't going to heal your arms," Richards grumbled as he threw the ball back to Jeremy.

"I know, but it may cool you off," Jeremy said in an attempt at humor.

"I don't have to put up with your lip, but if you want my help, you will take everything else that comes with it," Richards said.

"Yes sir," Jeremy replied.

"Now, last week, you did pitch fairly well, but you lost control," Richards avoided the direction their conversation had been heading.

"Right," Jeremy said downcast.

"We have two months until tryouts," he said. "That's not a lot of time. You have made progress, but we now have impromptu therapy to deal with, for your elbow and shoulder."

"I'll work harder," Jeremy interjected.

"You'll work smarter if you want to make it," Richards corrected. "You went too hard last week, which is part of the problem."

"I can do this," Jeremy said determined.

"Good," Richards said. "Let's get to work then."

-TWENTY-ONE-

"Is your Dad wearing a kilt?" Jeremy asked.

"Why yes, yes he is," Judy said looking in the kitchen to see her father cooking in a kilt. "He's proud of his heritage," she explained.

"And comfortable with his manhood," Jeremy commented.

"Or just comfortable enough to consider you family," Judy suggested.

"I haven't even proposed to you yet," Jeremy said flippantly, shocked at how easily it came.

"Are you going to ask?" Judy teased. "You still have said three little words yet."

Jeremy was saved from having to respond by the bounding family beagle jumping up to him. Jeremy quickly dropped their luggage on the entry floor to stop the dog from bowling him over. The noise of the dropped luggage attracted the attention of the family in the kitchen.

"Here they come," Judy laughed. "Ready?"

"As ready as I'll ever be," Jeremy muttered.

Jeremy was glad for this brief vacation. He had seen an increase in the strain of training over the last month. Richards was now volunteering his services to Jeremy every day of the week except for Sunday; Jeremy's only break in training. Richards ran alongside Jeremy as he swam laps yelling instructions on how to adjust his pull to best benefit his arms and shoulders. They spent odd days of the week in the weight room with Richards playing the part of the personal training and spotter.

Jeremy had been glad to get out of the state to visit Judy's family; it was a much needed break in the regime. Now that he was surrounded by Judy's five older brothers and two brothers-in-law, as well as sisters and sisters-in-law, he wasn't sure he had made the best decision.

He suspected that the giggling conversations Judy's sisters had with her were along the same lines as what he was ribbed about by the males of the family; would he be proposing. He didn't think that his response, "We're good friends, and she invited me here for the holiday," was holding any sway in the mind of her family.

Judy's father was very successful at whatever it was that he did. Their new home in Colorado's foothills was spacious. The house was spacious enough to fit nearly everyone in their own private nook of the home. Jeremy was excluded from the home because George insisted that Jeremy sleep in the guest bedroom of the pool house.

The apartment of the pool house was sparse. The family hadn't yet found a need to completely furnish the one-room accommodations. The room was above a billiard table room and changing room for the outdoor, heated swimming pool. Jeremy was able to have some privacy in the little apartment. A small fridge, sink, cabinets, table and futon bed were the only furniture in the upper room along with a bathroom, so he wouldn't have to share the shower and changing room downstairs. The majority of the one-room apartment was taken up by boxes that Judy's mother still had not unpacked since they moved in.

Even though it was the summer, the house lay in a crevice of the canyon hills of the Rockies. By late afternoon and into early evening, the air would cool quickly. By night, if Jeremy had left the windows open for too long, the futon bed and thin blanket were almost not enough to keep him warm. He normally liked a cool room when he slept, but being in unfamiliar territory unnerved him, especially since Judy's brothers tried to prank him by hog tying him and drag him into the pool on the first night.

Jeremy enjoyed the fourth, usually, no matter where he was. Although he didn't know her family, he enjoyed the closeness and the companionship they shared. As with most families, there was the occasional argument or scuffle. Some old issue would be brought up and dropped in a short-lived incident, replaced by sibling friendship. They attended a local parade in the morning, a barbeque for lunch, smoothies for dinner, and cuddling under blankets as one big family at the park grounds to watch the fireworks.

The women of the family were amazed at the sudden burst of energy in the men upon their return to the house late that night. The men insisted on a late night pool football match. Only George and a few of Judy's brothers were willing to have Jeremy sit out the game because of his arms and his training. However, a carefully-laid promise of a late night hog tie from the other brothers if he didn't join in was enough to convince Jeremy on his choice of late night activities.

An exhausting hour later, Jeremy climbed out of the heated pool, which no longer felt warm, to stand freezing in the air as he grabbed his towel. The more rambunctious of Judy's older brothers couldn't help themselves and dog piled Jeremy back into the pool. Disentangling the sodden towel from his arms and nursing a nearly broken nose, Jeremy laughed with the brothers, and they all went to their warm showers and beds. Jeremy had the slightest weakness of jealousy as he showered that they would not be going to bed alone.

Satisfied from an enjoyable, albeit long, day, Jeremy turned off the lights in the little apartment and slipped under the lone, thin blanket of the futon. He was actually fairly grateful for the pool football game; it just might have left him exhausted enough to not notice the slats of the futon through the mattress or how cold the apartment was from a faulty furnace that have never been replaced. Instead, the thing keeping him awake was a knocking at the door to the apartment.

Jeremy shuffled over and turned on the overhead light of the oven before opening the apartment door. Judy was standing on the other side, her hair pulled back in a tail, arms full with blankets and a bag.

"What are you doing?" Jeremy whispered.

"Coming for a visit," Judy responded and pushed her way into the apartment.

"Your parents will be pissed if you're here," Jeremy said, though he was glad she was taking the risk.

"Only Dad," Judy said, dumping the items on to the counter. "Mom likes you and probably won't mind us finally being able to spend some alone time during this break." She started to unpack cocoa mix and mugs from the bag. From under the counter, she pulled a rather abused looking pan for heating water. "I just thought you'd like some cocoa and extra blankets to keep you warm," she said with a blush that couldn't be hidden in the semidarkness.

"Thank you," Jeremy said as he helped spoon out cocoa mix.

"How's your nose by the way?" she asked over her shoulder.

"It's alright as long as I don't touch it," Jeremy said.

"Oh, I'm sorry," Judy said sympathetically. "I should have warned you better."

"Don't worry about it," he said simply. "I had fun."

"Good," she sounded relieved. "I had been worried."

"About whether I had fun?" Jeremy asked as he stirred the water.

"Well, that and if my family would be scaring you off," Judy admitted.

"Scaring me off from what?" he asked.

"Well, from," Judy shook her head. "I don't know."

"From saying I love you?" Jeremy said and saw Judy's fingers fumble with the cocoa.

"I guess," she didn't look at him.

"Well," he said as he poured hot water into the mugs. "I'm sure you wanted me to be comfortable with your family, and I suspect you would have liked to hear me say those words."

"Yes to both," she said accepting a mug. "And I understand if you have a hard time saying the words."

"I just said them," Jeremy said.

"But, that was different," Judy said pulling a blanket with her to sit on the futon.

"How so?" Jeremy teased.

"You have to mean the words," Judy said burning his lips on the cocoa. "You were just clarifying what I had been saying."

"Why don't you say them," Jeremy asked joining her on the bed. Judy wouldn't look at him. "You didn't want to scare me off?" he asked. She nodded. "Interesting."

"Interesting?" she blurted after swallowing the chocolate in her mouth. "All you can say is interesting?"

Laughing, Jeremy said, "You care so much about me and how I feel. What about you?"

"What about me?" she asked. "You're avoiding the conversation."

"So are you," Jeremy said.

"I had hoped that you had noticed how I've felt over these last few months," Judy said exasperated. "I won't say the words yet, because I'm afraid."

"Well, I was afraid as well," Jeremy admitted. "Afraid to admit how I felt. After I admitted it to myself, I was afraid that I was reading too much into how you felt about me. I didn't want to scare you off."

"So," she said slowly, "are you saying that we've been thinking the same thing and haven't said anything about it to each other."

"Like I said," Jeremy said. "Interesting."

"Well, you could have used a different phrase or word to describe it," she said huffing.

"Like what," he probed.

"I don't know," she said throwing one arm in the air, because she didn't want to spill her cocoa. "Wonderful, swell, anything corny that could give me more than interesting."

"Something like, I love you?" he asked with a smile.

"Stop doing that to me," she pouted and slumped against the wall, her knees pulled up to her chest. The baggy sleeves from her oversized hoody spilled over her hands. Her hair was coming loose from the tie and her face was hidden by the shadow of the window frame with the light of the moon resting only on the tip of her nose. "You know now how much I've wanted to hear those words from you and have you mean it."

"Yes. Just as much as I've wanted to mean it when and if I said them," he admitted.

"If?" Judy said downcast.

"When," Jeremy confirmed. "I just said that I knew it was how I felt about you."

"Then why haven't you said something before?" Judy said sitting up straight and kneeling in front of him. Her mug was empty of the cocoa and the chocolate was strong on her breath.

"I thought you would have wanted it said at some special occasion," Jeremy said.

"That only happens in stories," she said tucking her hair behind her ears. "Look at us. How often to you see people just talking about their feelings out in the open like this."

"It is kind of anticlimactic," Jeremy teased.

"Don't you say that," Judy slapped his arms. "I'm losing my mind here. You've been so close to saying it."

"I know," Jeremy looked away. "It's strange. I've never been so open with anyone in my life. I feel so comfortable around you that I could tell you anything. We're even talking about how strongly we feel for each other, and yet I'm still afraid of saying three simple words." He was standing now and pacing in front of the bed.

"It's okay," she said with emphasis. "It's not like those three words are a marriage proposal. Yes, it's a big thing to say and shouldn't be taken lightly."

"That's just the thing," Jeremy interjected.

"What is?" Judy asked, disarmed from being interrupted.

"I've become," he paused for the right word. "Very attached to your presence."

"We do spend a lot of time together," Judy said softly.

"Have I told you that I'm struggling with the whole baseball endeavor?" he asked.

"No, what do you mean?" she asked worriedly.

"Baseball doesn't hold the same fascination over me as it once did," Jeremy said. "I don't think about it all the time like I used to. All I think about is when I can be with you again."

"Jeremy," Judy whispered, struggling for air.

"It's true Judy," Jeremy said. "I have to say it. You know it's true, but you need to hear it." Jeremy waited and swallowed a number of times. "I can't stand the idea of not knowing where you and I will be. I love you."

"That wasn't so hard was it?" Judy teased.

"I expected you to be excited," Jeremy puzzled.

Judy smiled and put her hand on his cheek. "I am, but also surprisingly calm."

"This isn't how I expected this to happen," he chuckled. "I've never been here before and never really had anyone explain how this is supposed to be."

"I guess that is what you get for trying to learn the truth from television, movies, and books," Judy said softly.

"I guess so," Jeremy agreed. "So where do we go from here?"

"There's always marriage," Judy smiled.

"You haven't even said it back to me yet," Jeremy said incredulously. "And I thought there wasn't any pressure for that."

"It's true. There isn't," Judy teased. "But, you did say that you want to be together."

"Yes, but," Jeremy said getting hot.

"It's okay," Judy said. "You'll see the truth soon."

"You really do move fast once you start going," Jeremy scowled.

"We have technically been together for a year," Judy reminded. "We were just too stupid to admit anything until recently."

"So much wasted time," Jeremy commented. "We could have reached this point so long ago."

"It wasn't wasted," Judy said seriously. "It was what we needed."

"You're right," Jeremy smiled. "As usual."

"You are learning quickly," she smiled.

-TWENTY-TWO-

.

They continued to talk late into the night. They sat cross-legged across from each other with only their knees touching. They traded off with who went to refill mugs of cocoa until they were nearly sick of it.

"I'm amazed we are able to have so much to talk about," Jeremy commented at four in the morning.

"Are you saying you thought I was boring?" Judy glared at him.

"Not in the slightest," Jeremy back peddled. "I must have been boring to only talk about baseball."

"Yes, you were boring," she teased and smeared a melted mash mallow from her cocoa onto his nose. "I just had to get you to open up to me."

"I just meant that after being friends for over a year, I'm amazed there is so much we didn't know about each other," he said leaning back. "Should you be going?"

"Soon," Judy said glancing at the clock. "I am getting tired and I'd hate to fall asleep here and not make it back to my room until everyone woke up."

"That's true," Jeremy said. "I'd hate to see what you're brothers would do to me if they found out you spent the night here."

"Don't say it that way," Judy warned, "or they will think something happened."

"Still, how do we pass off why we are so exhausted?" Jeremy said.

"Well, hopefully they won't notice," Judy shrugged. "We are usually a laid back family the day after the fourth."

Leaning back forced Jeremy to acknowledge just how exhausted he really was. He flopped the rest of the way down. In moments, he was startled back awake as Judy was spreading a blanket over him.

"By the way," she said close to his ear. "I love you too."

A few hours later, after a late breakfast with the family, Jeremy sat on the couch in the main house with Judy snuggled into his shoulder falling asleep while the family went about the vacation plans for the day. Most of the kids were begging to be allowed to swim, so early in the day, but their parents were more reluctant to oblige.

Jeremy and Judy were saved from explaining anything; they and a few of Judy's siblings were watching the animated movie that was started for the kids, though the kids had long since lost interest. Jeremy's fingers were absently playing with Judy's hair before he'd caught himself and stopped. Judy's mother, Martha, kept giving them knowing glances whenever she passed. Judy wouldn't wakeup in his arms for him to ask if she had said anything to her mother that morning, so he was left to wonder on his own.

Judy woke in time for their lunch. Jeremy would have thought that someone would have commented on how tired he and Judy had been all morning, though no one did. As they sat down at the table eating silently and watching the family, Martha stuck her head between the two of them and put an arm around each.

"I'm so happy for you two," she said.

"What?" Jeremy asked.

"Mother!" Judy whined.

"Did you say something to her?" Jeremy hissed.

"She didn't need to," Martha said. "It's clear as day on your faces, but yes, she said something this morning."

"When?" Jeremy wanted to know.

"I woke her up this morning," Martha said gazing lovingly at her daughter. "She mumbled your name and sighed just before waking up. It only took a little prying to find out that you've moved onto the next step."

"What next step," a passing sibling said. "Did you finally propose?"

"No, they aren't engaged, they told us that when they arrived," another sister in law said.

"Well, he could have asked her last night," another said.

"No they could not have," growled George. "He didn't ask my permission yet."

"Dad, stop," Judy groaned.

"So he did ask?" demanded George.

"George, please," Martha said softly to stop the gossiping. "I was just giving them hypothetical motherly advice," she said as she gave a slight squeeze onto their shoulders as though to say, "There, I've got them under control again. Move at your own speed."

Jeremy was surprised on the following day when Judy's father supplied the family with tickets to a Rockies baseball game. The Rockies had been Jeremy's favorite team when he was younger. His oldest brother had given him a Rockies baseball hat for Christmas the year they were created. Jeremy immediately christened them his favorite team and had followed them throughout his life. Following the Rockies each season was Jeremy's justification for staying in touch with baseball, despite not playing on a team. Most of his limited knowledge of baseball rules and strategy had come from the commentators of the baseball games.

While most of the women in the family sat together to gossip, Jeremy was completely monopolized by the major league game. He occasionally joined in with the conversation with Judy's brothers, but only when they were discussing league standings or bad calls. Judy practically had to force his face away from the game to get him to accept the hot dog that was being passed down the row.

The weather was hot, but Jeremy did not mind the sweat, especially not when Judy would blow lightly on the back of his neck to cool him off. He was selfishly glad that Judy found the heat to be too much for cuddling during the game, because it would have been too uncomfortable. Everyone spent too much money on soda's and ice cream during the middle three innings when the heat reached a peak. They were located on the third base line with their backs to the setting sun. All of the women, Judy included, fussed over their significant others to put on more sun block to protect their necks from the Sun.

Despite the precautions, the men all had red necks by the time the game ended. They snacked in small groups after returning home and putting cranky, over tired, children to bed. The various couples trickled off to bed; Judy's father making a point to shepherd Judy off to bed while encouraging Jeremy to vacate to the pool house. Jeremy left the door of the pool house apartment unlocked, having caught a wink from Judy, and was not surprised when 45 minutes later, Judy snuck in with more hot chocolate, aloe, and a box of photo albums.

Judy kept Jeremy up late into the night with photos and albums spread across the floor and bed. Judy found some method to the madness in the spread as she chronicled the captured events and stories in the photos.

"That would have been good to know before I came up," Jeremy said after Judy hastily covered photographs of an old high school fling.

As the stories ran late into the night, Jeremy found increasing opportunities to share his own stories that were similar to Judy's life. Every hour Judy would lather more aloe burn gel on Jeremy's neck, face, ears, and forearms. She would blow on the gel to get it to dry faster and cool off his skin; Jeremy could only squirm as the raising hairs on the back of his neck would stand on end.

After a long night, and far too many cups of chocolate, they kissed goodnight, lingered too long, and fell asleep for what few hours remained of the night.

"I'm not sure what to make of the numerous questions about if we are going to get married," Jeremy admitted part-way through their drive back to the university on Sunday. "Or what to take from their reactions."

"Well, I am one of the youngest in the family," Judy began, "they like to give me a hard time, but I think they all liked you."

"Or were just being nice to the guest," grouched Jeremy.

"No, my brothers are not that nice," Judy admitted. "Give yourself some credit and stop doubting your worth. They've never liked anyone I've brought over. The fact that they liked you and invited you along to so many things means a lot."

"Okay, I'll believe you, because I'm too tired to argue," Jeremy conceded and received a playful slap on his arm.

The rest of the drive was slow and relaxing. They only had a six-hour drive and took their time to stop at scenic pull offs on the freeway. They had an early dinner, leftovers provided by Judy's mother, and napped for a few minutes before continuing their drive.

They arrived back at campus after dark, thoroughly exhausted. Jeremy remarked that he found it odd that for a vacation he got less sleep than he normal did during a school weeks. Judy kissed his cheek and reminded him that the sleep deprivation was not stress-induced and had been rather enjoyable and fulfilling.

-TWENTY-THREE-

For the remainder of the two months until the tryouts, Jeremy longed to return to the pool house and spend endless nights with Judy. He was losing his desire in training, despite the constant encouragement from Judy. He still wanted to fight to make it to tryouts but was faced with discouragement.

Jeremy felt that he was hitting his plateau in speed and form. Training blended into one long nightmare. Richards was increasingly more stern and short with him. His parents found out that he had been spending his free time training for a sports team instead of taking extra classes to finish his degree. They accused him of throwing away a perfect chance at a good education to play a game. Judy was his only relief and support, but he could not go to her all the time for support; he always felt that he should be spending the time he had with her building their relationship, instead of on his woes with baseball training.

Shortly after the vacation to Judy's home, Jeremy moved into an attic apartment above an elderly couple; Mr. and Mrs. Kiplinger. His rent was cheap after negotiating yard work duties for the house. The attic apartment reminded Jeremy of the single-room apartment above the pool house at Judy's home in Colorado. He was furnished with a small fridge, sink, and stove. The elderly couple insisted that he join them for dinners on most nights, so his fridge rarely had anything other than breakfast foods. Mrs. Kiplinger treated Jeremy as though he was her only grandson and son rolled into one person. She positively twittered whenever Judy came to visit Jeremy. Judy, in turn, became so enamored with Mrs. Kiplinger that the two would spend Sunday afternoons baking while Jeremy took long naps in the hammock and Mr. Kiplinger dozed on the back porch chair with a book in his lap.

Jeremy was pitching more throughout the week. His arms hurt constantly, and he felt like he couldn't sleep well. Every morning, Richards would be waiting in his car outside Jeremy's apartment and drive behind him as Jeremy ran. Then, they would head over to the all-day gym and go through some light resistance training on Jeremy's legs and arm.

Once the regular semester started back up, Jeremy would go to his classes while Richards went to his job. At the end of the day, after Jeremy had some time to study, Richards would be done with his job and dinner with is family and would meet Jeremy to either pitch or swim laps. They had to get special permission from the school facilities to let Richards walk along the side of the pool to yell at Jeremy as he swam.

Judy began to accompany Jeremy to the practice sessions; it was her only way of being able to see Jeremy during the week. At first, Richards vocally disapproved of the idea. However, Judy kept out of the way and was able to learn some basic sports physical therapy from Richards to help Jeremy during their breaks.

As the fall began to settle in, Jeremy grew more nervous as he approached the tryouts. Judy and Jeremy occasionally saw Steve on campus or playing a pickup game of football at the park in the neighboring field to the diamond. Steve had grown to finally acknowledging not only their presence in the world but also their relationship. The most recognition they received was the slightest head nod from Steve.

Jeremy would later regret how he treated Judy during the beginning of the fall semester. He was so strained from school and training that he was becoming more distracted and short-tempered. Unfortunately, he began to take this out on Judy. She stayed up late with him to help him with his homework on top of her weighty work load. He finally came to grips with how poorly he was treating her when a late night argument resulted in tears from Judy.

"I am so sorry," Jeremy pleaded. "I'll stop this whole baseball nonsense."

"It's not that," Judy said through some tissues.

"Yes, it is," Jeremy insisted. "It's been monopolizing my time on and off the diamond, and I'm not even on a team."

"It's your dream," Judy stomped her foot. "I don't want to be the cause of you not reaching a dream."

"You wouldn't be the one stopping me from this dream," Jeremy said. "It's not the only dream I have for life."

"Jeremy, you have worked so hard for this," Judy tried to reason with him.

"Judy, having this dream come true would not be worth anything if I lost our relationship," Jeremy said softly.

"You'd move on," Judy sniffled.

"Maybe, after a long time," Jeremy said. "But, I'd never be happy. I could never be happy knowing I hurt and lost you. I'd never be as happy, because they wouldn't be you."

"I don't want you to give up on this," Judy said fiercely.

"I don't want this if it isn't with you," Jeremy pleaded. "I know you have given so much to help me. I know you at the limit of all you can give. Please let me do this for you."

"Jeremy, you didn't listen to me," Judy had stopped crying. "I want you to go through with this. I don't want you to have any regrets about this experience. You beat yourself up too much about lost opportunities in your life. Don't add another one."

"But, I…" Jeremy began.

"I know you don't want to lose me either," Judy held up a hand to stop him. "So that won't happen. I love you Jeremy. We are just being tested through all of this strain. Can we survive the test? I'd like to," she said softly.

"Me too," Jeremy agreed. "This is just a reminder to not take you for granted."

"Exactly," Judy said with a smile. "See, that wasn't so bad."

"It wasn't so great either," Jeremy admitted. "I don't like arguing with you."

"So don't," teased Judy. "We're not married, we're just a couple. That gives us some breathing room, but even if we were married, it is okay to have different opinions and interests. We can have disagreements; let's just try to not let them escalate to arguments."

"I'll try harder," Jeremy said.

"I know," Judy said. "We both will."

-TWENTY-FOUR-

Finally, the time to put his name on the list for tryouts arrived. "Well, that's over and done with," Jeremy sighed as he exited the athletic building to meet Judy.

"No turning back now," Judy said gathering her belongings.

"I only turned in the information sheet about me and the position I'll be trying out for. I can still not show up," Jeremy pointed out.

"Like that would happen," Judy snorted in mock laughter.

"You're right. I just have to survive two more days," Jeremy said.

"How are you going to spend the time?" Judy asked.

"Richards wants me to keep my arm loose for the next few days. I am not to pitch hard, but I can toss the ball just to keep it loose," Jeremy explained.

"You can throw but not pitch?" confirmed Judy.

"Yep."

"Hmm. Then, in that case," Judy said thinking. "I've got an idea."

Judy had Jeremy lead her back to their apartments and gather both of his mitts and a ball. "Here, you take the lefty because there is no way I can catch with a lefty mitt," Judy explained. "I'll use your right glove."

"You're cute," Jeremy smiled as he backed off. "I'd have to say that this is the first time I've ever seen you play catch."

"Yeah, it's been a while since I've done this," she admitted with a proud shrug. "Too bad having you throw left isn't a handy-cap."

"Yep, we should have done this months ago," he said still backing up.

"That's too far," Judy warned. "I'll never reach that far."

"We'll work you up to it," he smiled and tossed the ball.

"This is actually pretty relaxing," Judy admitted after a few minutes.

"You sound surprised," Jeremy chuckled. "Would Steve have been willing to do this if it wasn't relaxing?"

"Well, you both are weird," she caught the ball awkwardly. "I'll admit that I never did understand the fascination you guys have with this sport."

"Don't tell me. It's boring," Jeremy mimicked.

"Yes, actually," she tried to throw it back hard, but Jeremy didn't show any difficulty in catching the ball. "I couldn't stand it before, but, well, if the company I'm with is good," she smiled.

"Of course," he said, tossing it back to her and making her reach.

"So, are you going to be upset if you don't make the team?" Judy asked.

"Even though I don't want to admit it, yes, I would be," he paused before throwing again. "Of course I'll be upset because of all the hard work I've put in, but" he sighed as he caught the ball. "I did get into this just so that I could say that I've tried. I'll try my hardest trying to make the team, but I'm going to have to try hard not to be heartbroken when they cut me."

"If they cut you," Judy responded with heavy emphasis on if.

"Of course; if," Jeremy contemplated.

Two days later, Jeremy was nervously standing in front of the sign in table for tryouts. He accepted the number to pin to his shirt and listened carefully to the instructions he was given about tryouts.

Jeremy found his way over to the prospective pitchers and could easily tell that he may be out of his league. There were a number of pitchers that were clearly returning players. Jeremy tried to block everything from his mind and stretch his arms as he walked over to check in at the pitching station to be told his order in the tryouts.

Almost immediately after checking in, he heard a familiar voice, "Welcome prospective pitchers. I am Coach Thompson," the head coached called out. "I'll be watching your tryouts personally while my other coaching staff focuses on other positions.

"We have already recruited a few prospective pitchers. What we want here today is to find a few more possibilities that we may have missed in recruiting and to give past players an opportunity to switch positions," he acknowledged the few returning players. "There are no guarantees for anything other than if you have signed your name, you will be given a time to pitch. Even if you are called onto the team, that does not mean you will play, but you will be used as much as possible and needed."

Jeremy watched the coach walk off with some assistants as they prepared the list of pitchers. Jeremy stood off to the side near the other pitchers and continued stretching his arms.

"Hey, I'm Greg," said a dark skinned, smiling, and pitcher next to him.

"Jeremy," Jeremy said with a nod as they were both stretching.

"Where'd you play ball?" Greg asked.

"Just here and there," Jeremy shrugged avoiding his eyes.

"Good one," Greg chuckled and switched stretches. "No, seriously."

"Um, intramurals and pickup city games," Jeremy said sheepishly.

"You serious? And you're trying out?" Greg asked.

"Yep," Jeremy said trying to sound more confident than he felt.

"Well, good luck," Greg said. "You're either really good or really brave."

"Thanks for not saying stupid," Jeremy smiled.

"Well, that remains to be seen, but you look serious enough," Greg said.

"What about you? How long have you played?" Jeremy asked.

"High school team," he said. "I wasn't recruited, but I think I've got a shot."

"At least they'll look at us," Jeremy said watching the first pitcher on the mound. "That's all I can ask for."

"Yeah, I just hate the phone call," Greg said.

"The phone call?"

"Yeah, they call no matter what; yes or no," Greg said.

"They call you to say no?" Jeremy asked again. "That's got to be nerve racking."

"You have no idea," Greg shook his head. "But, you'll learn."

Jeremy watched the other pitchers as the tryouts progressed. He tried to subtly copy their methods of staying warm and loose until their turn came to pitch. He noticed that there did not seem to be a set number of pitches but rather you pitched until the coaches said stop.

"Number fourteen?" an assistant called out an hour later. Jeremy ran up to the table for the coaches.

"You'll be asked to pitch a series of pitches until the coaches say stop. You will not be told the results of your try out at this time," she droned.

"Um, I actually have a question," he interrupted. I am actually trying out for both hands. Do I do both hands now or do I wait and do the other later?"

"I uh. I have no idea," she admitted looking over at the coaches.

"You are doing what?" one assistant coach asked.

"I put on my information sheet that I pitch left and right and would like to try out that way," Jeremy repeated.

"You're serious?" the assistant coach asked.

"Yes sir," Jeremy said with a nod and produced both mitts.

The assistant coach laughed, "Hey Doug, you've got to hear this," he motioned over Coach Thompson.

"What is it?" the head coach asked.

"This kid here wants to show us how he can pitch with both hands," the assistant coach said through more laughter.

"I'm sorry son," Coach Thompson started. "Only one hand allowed." Then he looked at Jeremy and paused. "Wait, aren't you the one that came to see me last spring?"

"Yes sir. I did sir," Jeremy said.

"And what did I say?" the coach asked.

"Pretty much the same thing your assistant coach said," Jeremy replied.

"We only want to see one hand. So pick one," Coach Thompson said.

"But, I can do both," Jeremy insisted.

"Look kid," the assistant coach butted in. "We don't care if you can pitch while singing the National Anthem. If you want to try out, you pick a hand."

"I'm not wasting your time, so let me do this," Jeremy said getting angry. The coaches stiffened as his outburst. "I know you wouldn't even consider me if I didn't have something unique. I do have some-thing unique. I can pitch with either hand. I don't get tired as easily as your normal pitchers, because I have been training to withstand pain and fatigue from both arms.

"When I do get tired, I just switch hands. I can handle any batter that comes my way and eliminate some of their advantage of being left or right."

"Tell you what," Coach Thompson said. "If you can prove to us that you are just as good with either hand, we'll consider your tryout seriously and not as some kind of a joke."

"The best proof is the real deal," Jeremy said squaring up. "I'll do one pitch each hand and then focus on whichever one you want before showing more of the other," and he walked off to the mound. "Catcher! Let's go," Jeremy called as he went. The catcher looked at the coaching table for instructions and was given the wave to continue.

Without even putting on either glove, Jeremy grabbed a ball from the basket by the mound and squared up with is left shoulder to home plate. He angrily wound up and delivered a fastball that couldn't have been better if he'd wanted. Then, with just enough time for the catcher to throw the ball back, Jeremy had caught the ball bare handed, switched directions and pitched his left hand with just the same amount of strength.

Jeremy didn't look to the coaches for confirmation or instruction and continued to pitch back and forth; left then right, all the while only catching with his bare hands. His hands stung as he pitched, and finally, after ten minutes of switching, he was instructed to stop. "Right first," one of the coaches hollered and Jeremy noticed that the other pitchers and many of the other stations around the field had stopped to watch him.

After 30 consecutive fast balls with his right hand, the coaches wanted to see a few of his curveballs. Ten pitches later and with a right hand that was beginning to tingle, the coaches yelled for him to switch to his left. Now Jeremy could see in his peripheral vision the coaches table. As he continued to pitch nearly the same number of pitches with his left, he felt himself get into that ultra-concentrated rhythm of pitching. His breathing and pitching were harmonious. No matter what the outcome, this was the best he had ever done with both arms.

Jeremy had been on the mound for a straight 40 minutes, pitching, when the coaches finally called out, "That's enough."

Relieved to be finished, Jeremy saw that many of the assistant looked impressed, but Coach Thompson was scowling as he turned to some returning players that were taking a break from their tryouts. "Adams," Thompson yelled. "Get a bat and hustle over here."

"Coach?" Jeremy asked.

Turning to Jeremy, he said, "Son, you've shown you can throw by switching every time for a while now. Then, we had you pitch straight for 40 minutes with each arm.

"Now, I want you to pitch against one of our best. You need to strike him out first with your right hand, then with you left," Thompson ordered.

"Yes sir," Jeremy nodded.

The player named Adams lined up at the plate. The catcher signaled a pitch. Jeremy, felt more calm than he would have expected in this situation and pitched three perfect strikes; fastball, curve, fastball. Adams went out swinging to Jeremy's right hand.

"Now left," the coach yelled.

Jeremy switched gloves and shook out his arms.

"It's like watching a completely different pitcher," the assistant coach said to Thompson. "It's remarkable."

Coach Thompson could only grunt in response as he watched Jeremy pitch against Adams with his left hand. The first two were strikes. The last pitch, Adams connected and sent a pop fly to the outfield. Another one of the pitchers who was waiting for his turn ran out and caught the ball.

"I thought you were trying out for pitcher not the outfield," yelled Coach Thompson to the pitcher who caught the fly ball. Many of the other players chuckled.

Jeremy collected his gloves and jogged, disappointedly, back to the coaches table.

"Well, it was an out," the assistant coach smiled, impressed at what he had just witnessed.

"But, not what I asked for," Coach Thompson frowned.

"I know sir," Jeremy said.

"I don't want a pitcher who can't deliver what I want. I don't want someone talking back to me," he said trying to deny the impressive display.

"Yes sir," Jeremy said promptly. "With all due respect, I needed the chance."

"Yeah well, you've proved you're adept as a pitcher, but you're going to have to wait like everyone else for the result," Coach Thompson said, looking at his clipboard.

"That's fair. I just needed you to watch me once," Jeremy said graciously. "Thank you for the opportunity," he said before jogging off to collect his belongings and leave the field.

-TWENTY-FIVE-

"So, it has been two weeks," Judy said as she walked with Jeremy. "They're supposed to call today."

"They are?" Jeremy asked sarcastically. "I didn't know that."

Judy slapped his arm, "Aren't you even nervous?"

"No more than I was two weeks ago at tryouts," Jeremy admitted.

"Have you talked to Mr. Richards?" Judy asked.

"Yeah, I called him right after tryouts to tell him how I thought they went," Jeremy said. "He was surprisingly kind."

"I thought he was always kind with you?" Judy asked puzzled.

"He was," Jeremy admitted. "I just had thought for the last two months that he was bugged with me, like I had lost his trust because of pitching against Steve."

"What was he like on the phone?"

"He said he was proud of me," Jeremy said softly. "He said he didn't like being so stern with me, but that I needed a coach more than a mentor at that moment, and he wished me the best."

"Is he interested in finding out if you make the team?" she asked.

"Of course. He said he'd let me be his assistant coach if I don't make the team," Jeremy smiled.

"Well, that's something," Judy said.

"Yep. You know what they say. Those who can, do. Those who can't, teach," Jeremy shrugged in resignation.

"I know," she said, pulling herself closer to him and pressing herself against his arm.

They walked the rest of the way to his apartment in silence. They entered the apartment and found it empty. After dumping their bags on the table and their coats over the kitchen chairs, they slumped onto the couch. Jeremy played with his phone a little before tossing it onto the coffee table.

"When are they supposed to call?" Judy asked again, clearly as anxious as Jeremy.

"Sometime today is all I know," Jeremy responded.

At that moment, the phone rang. Judy sprang for it and answered it for him, "Hello?" she said. "Just a moment," and she handed the phone to Jeremy mouthing with a concerned expression, "It's the coach."

-EPILOGUE-

Fall progressed into winter, and with it, torrential snows. Jeremy complained about how wet the ends of his pants would get in the melting snow. He slipped often on the ice and slush patches on campus while Judy maintained the grace of a figure skater as she flittered across the snow, beaming with each snow flake that fell on her face.

Jeremy spent Thanksgiving and part of the Christmas break with Judy and her family; they were closer than his parents who were visiting family on the East Coast. After the Christmas break, Judy and Jeremy started the winter semester of their junior year of college.

Winter passed slowly into a cold spring, and the college baseball season started once again. Jeremy and Judy were holding hands as they walked between the campus buildings on the day of the first game of the new college season.

"So, remember," Judy reminded Jeremy yet again. "My class runs late today and I've got to meet with my group for a bit afterwards." She turned to Jeremy. "I know that it's important to be there for the National Anthem, and I'll try not to be late."

"I know you'll be on time," Jeremy smiled.

"Thanks," she stood on her toes to kiss him. "I'll see you there then."

"See you later," Jeremy said. "Don't fall asleep in class."

"I'll try not to," Judy said with a look that clearly said she wouldn't be upset if she did fall asleep.

That afternoon, as the sun was nearing the mountains in the west, Judy arrived at the stadium just before the National Anthem with a blanket around her arms. She hurried up to their spot from the previous year and settled in, looking for Jeremy. Instead, she saw Steve coming up the bleachers and waved him over. "Hi Steve!"

"Hey Judy." He said. "Did I miss the starting lineup?"

"Nope," she said brushing her hair.

"I heard the good news," he said pointing to her left hand.

"Oh yeah? Thanks," she beamed looking at the engagement ring Jeremy had given her the month before.

"I'm happy for you," Steve said softly. "I really am."

"Thanks," Judy said. "That means a lot."

"Do you mind if I join you?" he asked.

"Not at all," she moved to let him slip past her. "I know Jeremy will be glad to see you here."

"Yeah, he's getting tired of my apologies," Steve sighed.

"Of course he is," Judy said with a kind laugh. "You're his friend and he doesn't want to think about what happened anymore."

"Good, I guess." Steve muttered.

"I hope it doesn't get too cold," Judy said.

"It is only mid-March. It does usually get cold for these first few home games," Steve said.

"I know," Judy said still looking for Jeremy. "I can hope."

"Yeah, you do that and let me know how it turns out," Steve laughed.

Before Judy could respond, the announcer came over the speakers, "Please stand and welcome your team as they meet at the mound for the National Anthem."

Everyone cheered and Judy stood to clap still looking for Jeremy.

"There he is," Steve said pointing.

They could both see a familiar form on the field as Jeremy jogged out with the rest of the team to the mound. He proudly sported a number fourteen on his back and waved his hat to Judy and Steve before placing it over his heart to face the flag over the outfield wall.

THE END

ACKNOWLEDGEMENTS

Thank you family for being patient with me as I wrote and re-wrote. I'd like to thank everyone that told me about National Novel Writing Month and for introducing me to something that helped me get this story out of my head. Thanks to all my fellow NaNoWriMo participants for sharing your enthusiasm and encouragement. Thank you Steve, for helping me come up with this idea years ago and letting me use your name. I may be mostly ambidextrous, but I am more like Steve and you are the real Jeremy. A very big thank you to Hans Zimmer, John Williams, Nicholas Hooper, Jack Johnson, Beethoven, Patrick Doyle, and Yo-Yo Ma. Your wonderful works of music helped me write and overcome many days of writer's block.

AUTHOR NOTE

Stories have always been an important aspect of my life. My earliest memories were of my father reciting The Jabberwocky from Lewis Carroll, or my mother reading classic literature or poetry to the family such as the Song of Hiawatha.

While I loved stories, I rarely wanted to read and never wanted to write anything of my own. I was remarkably changed by two teachers. The first was my fourth grade reading teacher who helped me find a love for reading. I began reading so much that my reading level and comprehension jumped from remedial to an advanced level in a year. Later, in High School, I was assigned to write a short, two-page story for my English class. That night, I wrote 18 pages of a story that had been in my head for over a year. From that point, I wanted to bring life to the stories in my head.

I stopped writing when I started college. I was too busy trying to pass my classes while having some semblance of a social life to spend any time with creative writing. When I spent two years in Massachusetts, half way through college, I woke one night from a terrible and intriguing dream. I couldn't sleep for the rest of the night, and I was distracted all the next day thinking about my dream. The following night, I fixed an old typewriter that was stored in the cluttered basement of the house that I was staying in. I started to write about my dream and it slowly developed from a journal entry, to a narrative, and then into a story idea.

Over the months remaining in my time in Massachusetts, whenever I couldn't sleep, I would go into the front room and would add more to the growing story. Writing became a therapy for my nightmares and fears. Writing helped me cope with the trials during the day. Writing for only an hour each night for the last six months in Massachusetts, I had completed my largest, continuous stream of writing ever; over 30,000 words. The plot is far too depressing for me to ever finish; not for want of trying. It has been six years since I started the idea. I have tried to convert it into a digital form and finish the story, but I know that it would be better to leave the story unfinished.

When I returned to college, I thought that I would want to study film because of my love of stories and my frustration and feeling like I could never adequately tell the story in print.

My friend and neighbor, Steve, and I loved watching baseball movies, baseball games, and going to our college baseball games while trying to maintain our grades. We thought that while you see switch hitters, you never see a switch pitcher. We toyed around with the idea of how effective a switch pitcher would be and how hard it would be to train as a switch pitcher. I used this idea for a five-minute script assignment for a film class. In the end, I was not accepted into the film program and had to find a different undergraduate degree.

After a lot of research and debate, I decided on sociology, largely because it was the shortest degree and one in which I held a marginal interest. Most of my classes did not hold my interest to the point of wanting to pursue sociology beyond an undergraduate degree. In my sociology theory night class, I was struggling to stay awake when a random image came to my head. I opened a new document on my laptop and began to furiously type. The result was the beginning of a project in which I am rather invested and hopeful. By the time I was introduced to the National Novel Writing Month 2009 competition, my project had been two years in the running and far too developed to be used for the competition. The Switch Pitcher was an experiment in two parts. I currently have a number of projects that I am writing, most of which are in the fantasy or science fiction genre. However, when National Novel Writing Month was recommended to me, I decided to give it a try. I had to use an idea that I was not currently writing. I also wanted to see if I could write a complete novel from start to finish in a month. I resurrected the old five-page script idea from film class about a kid who was a switch pitcher.

During the month of November 2009, I churned out a new idea, based on the simple idea of a kid wanting to play for his college team by pitching with both arms. National Novel Writing Month was an interesting endeavor, not only due to starting and finishing a complete novel in the space of 30 days, but also for the challenge of writing a novel in the general fiction genre, completely devoid of robots, spaceships, or anything else that is common in my favorite genres.

Encouraged by my completion of this novel, I am even more anxious to return to the project I started while I was finishing my sociology degree in 2007. I hope that this will be the beginning of a wonderful, albeit challenging, endeavor.